"Let me get this clear," she said carefully. "You want to marry *me*?"

"It's a solution. For us both."

It wasn't romantic. It was cut-and-dried, black-and-white: a business arrangement.

"Before I make a decision, I'll need to know what, exactly, the marriage entails."

A flash of the passion in the front seat of his truck briefly welded her to the spot, but that heat dissipated as Damon briefly outlined the main points.

Basically, it was a matter of sharing his River Oaks mansion in Houston for a couple of months. Other than that, she could continue her life as usual, just as he would.

"So all we do is *share* your mansion."

"As a legally married couple."

"I think I need a little more detail than that, because it's a fact that whenever you and I get together, we usually do a whole lot more than share space." She met his gaze squarely and took the bull by the horns. "What happens if we make love?"

Heat flared in his gaze. It was gone so quickly that, if they hadn't kissed earlier, she might almost have thought she had imagined it. But they *had* kissed, which meant that, however reluctant he was to admit it, Damon did still want her.

The thought made her go still inside and, suddenly, her mind was made up.

Two months with Damon.

Dear Reader,

When I started out writing, my first hero was a down-under cowboy and a bad boy with a troubled past and a heart of gold, so it feels a little like coming full circle to write another bad-boy cowboy, although this time he is also a billionaire and oil tycoon.

Damon Wyatt is tough and alpha, a protector with a self-deprecating sense of humor. He's also determined not to fall in love so, when he's forced by the terms of his uncle's will to marry, of course he solves that dilemma by contracting a marriage of convenience fenced in by more rules than you can poke a stick at...and not to the woman he really wants.

Enter Jenna Beaumont, Damon's ex: a Southern debutante with a wedding planning business. Stranded with Damon in a storm when Damon's contracted bride can't make the wedding, Jenna becomes Damon's only marriage option. And she knows exactly what to do with his marriage rules.

Break *all* of them.

I hope you enjoy it!

Best wishes and every blessing,

Fiona

FIONA BRAND

PLAYING BY THE MARRIAGE RULES

Thank you, as always, to my editor, Stacy Boyd, who, with her usual care and creativity, really helped make this story shine.

Recycling programs for this product may not exist in your area.

ISBN-13: 978-1-335-73556-0

Playing by the Marriage Rules

Harlequin Enterprises ULC
22 Adelaide St. West, 41st Floor
Toronto, Ontario M5H 4E3, Canada
www.Harlequin.com

Printed in U.S.A.

Fiona Brand lives in the Bay of Islands, New Zealand. Aside from being the mother of two real-life heroes, her sons, Fiona likes to read the Bible, garden, cook, socialize with friends and travel. After a life-changing encounter, she continues to walk with God, is a priest in the Anglican Church and a member of the Order of St. Luke, Christ's Healing Ministry. And she "finally" has her Bachelor of Theology.

Books by Fiona Brand

Harlequin Desire

Playing by the Marriage Rules
How to Live with Temptation

The Pearl House

A Breathless Bride
A Tangled Affair
A Perfect Husband
The Fiancée Charade
Just One More Night
Needed: One Convenient Husband
Twin Scandals
Keeping Secrets

Visit her Author Profile page
at Harlequin.com for more titles.

You can also find Fiona Brand on Facebook,
along with other Harlequin Desire authors,
at Facebook.com/harlequindesireauthors.

To the Lord, who helps me with all things.
Thank you!

The gift of God is eternal life through
Jesus Christ our Lord.

—*Romans* 6:23

One

Damon Wyatt had to marry by midnight.

If he was still single when the clock struck twelve, his uncle Alan's entire fortune would be passed down to a distant cousin who owned a car dealership in Florida. All the years Damon had invested studying business management, working as a roughneck for his eccentric uncle's oil company and as a hand on Alan Wyatt's sprawling ranch—learning the business from the ground up—would have been for nothing.

Ducking through driving rain, Damon strode into the exclusive country lodge Alan had "provisionally" left him, along with the rest of the Wyatt ranching and oil conglomerate. His jaw tightened at the terms of the will that he had spent the last year attempting to overturn. He understood why his great-uncle, the only Wyatt in recent family history who had experienced a happy marriage—albeit a childless one—was using the leverage of the will to force him into marriage. Alan knew Damon's history only too well, since he was the one who had stepped in and rescued him at age sixteen from the violence and dysfunction that had characterized his father's marriage to a wealthy heiress. Even so, Damon had long ago decided that marriage was not for him. His uncle had won this round—Damon would marry—but it would be on *his* terms, which was a paper marriage for the minimum period of two months and no more.

He dropped his overnight bag by the front desk just as Caleb Jones, his legal counsel, who had flown in from Houston, stepped out of a room off to the right.

"You're here, *finally*—"

"My flight into San Antonio was delayed. What's the emergency?"

Caleb jerked his head at the room he'd just exited. "That's the emergency."

Damon frowned at the room, which appeared to be decorated with white roses and glossy green foliage, as Mark Hennessey, a tall, thick-set guy with a bald head, who looked more like a prizefighter than the manager of a luxury lodge, joined them. "I see you've found our wedding venue," Hennessey said grimly. He consulted a clipboard he was carrying under one arm. "Your—uh, bride, Ms. North, hired a wedding planner. Some relative of hers."

An automatic tension gripped Damon as Hennessey handed him an expensive-looking pamphlet made of heavy cream parchment. How many wedding planner relatives could the convenient bride he had contracted to marry him just ten days ago possibly have?

Answer: only one.

To be more precise, the one he had slept with for two months before he had been forced to end the addictive liaison with gorgeous, high-maintenance Jenna Beaumont so he could contract a controllable, convenient bride in time to meet his marriage deadline.

Damon flipped the pamphlet open and an all-too-familiar light floral fragrance made every muscle in his body tighten. Jenna's name leaped off the page, and the passionate relationship he'd known was a mistake from the first, an irresistible mistake—*just like all the other ones*—rushed back at Damon with all the force of a freight train.

Magnetic blue eyes, exotic cheekbones and a firm jaw, sleek dark blond hair, and the kind of taut, curvy body and elegant stroll that had turned heads, including his, for more years than he could count...

Jenna was the gorgeous, pampered daughter of one of the oldest and most prestigious families in Texas. A Southern debutante who might take a walk on the wild side with him but, when it came to marriage, would always follow her family's proud tradition and marry money.

The kind of girl whom, when he'd had little more

than a truck and a saddle—and the kind of past that had made people from the wealthy side of town cross the road to avoid him—he shouldn't have gone near. But he had made the mistake of doing just that, and more. And not once, but *three* times.

The last time had been just three months ago, when he had crossed paths with Jenna at an uptown restaurant in Houston. Those casual encounters had been happening with a disturbing regularity ever since he had moved to Houston a year ago but, on that occasion, he had fallen into a familiar trap. After watching her coolly fend off some slick lawyer who had decided that their dinner date should end in his apartment, he had finally given in to temptation and had stepped in to rescue her.

After dispatching the lawyer, instead of walking away, he had made the fatal mistake of cutting his own business meeting short, then had insisted on dropping Jenna home just in case her disgruntled date tried to follow her.

When he had seen her to her door, that first mistake had been compounded by a second. One kiss, memories that had flowed hot and fast, and a slow walk through moonlit rooms to her bed, and six years of hard-won abstinence had dissolved.

He had found himself once more caught in the grip of a destructive mismatch with a spoiled heiress that was a carbon copy of the mistake his father had made, and which had been his own personal tour of hell as a child. The kind of out-of-control, emotional relationship he was normally careful to avoid because he'd had his fill of hurt.

Despite that, he had still been crazily tempted to propose that Jenna should be his convenient bride… until he had realized that she was angling to marry him for real.

Broodingly, he refolded the scented pamphlet and slipped it into his jacket pocket. He had managed to walk away, just, but his mistake in getting involved with Jenna again had come back to bite him when she had discovered that he had been seen out with another woman. As it happened, the first bride he had selected.

Overnight, the details of their quiet liaison, which could only have been supplied by Jenna, had exploded across a prominent blogger's social media platforms. A day later, his sedate thirtysomething bride had walked, leaving him with the comment that she was just in it for the money, not the sex.

With just two weeks to his deadline, he'd been forced to start the selection process again. But, with his reputation now scorched, finding a suitable candidate—one who didn't want two months with the Houston stallion *and* the cash—had proved problematic.

Out of viable options, when Caleb's socialite ex, Chloe, had offered to help him out, he had settled for her. Unfortunately, she also happened to be Jenna's cousin.

Looking irritable and on edge, Caleb jerked his head in the direction of the room he'd just exited.

"Before you do anything else, you need to check out that room."

Jaw tight, Damon followed Caleb and Hennessey through double glass doors into a spacious room—and stopped dead.

Once filled with dark leather sofas and low coffee tables, with hunting trophies decorating the walls, and a bar at one end, the room—now devoid of the trophies—was literally smothered in white roses. Swags of ivory-white tulle were draped to frame the ranks of bifold doors, and lavish groupings of white candles occupied the once-empty open fireplace and were arranged on almost every available coffee table. Just yards away, a table was set for a romantic dinner for two, with silverware, champagne glasses, a lush centerpiece of candles and roses, and pristine white linen.

It could now only be described as the last thing on earth Damon ever wanted to see: a high-end wedding venue.

Caleb folded his arms over his chest. "Please tell me this is still a marriage of convenience."

"You know it is," Damon growled.

The agreement with Chloe had been clear-cut. The marriage was little more than a business arrangement, and he could have sworn she was just as objective as he was about it. One of the reasons he had chosen her—aside from desperation—was that, as one of Caleb's numerous exes, during the few occasions they'd socialized, she had barely noticed him.

That was exactly the quality Damon was looking for in a convenient bride.

His mood dropping by the second, he scanned the room, which had clearly cost a small fortune to put together.

Was that a *wedding arch* in the corner?

Absently, Damon set his briefcase down on a nearby sideboard that had once been used to hold a whiskey decanter and glasses. It was now a repository for glass-canopied cake stands loaded with cupcakes, topped with swirls of white buttercream icing and tiny bride and groom figures.

He transferred his gaze to Hennessey. "You should have called me."

"I would have," he said gloomily, "if I'd known this was going to happen. But I've been away for a couple of days myself. When I got in this morning it was like the place had been taken over by ninjas, they moved so fast."

Looking like his world had been violated, Hennessey detached a booklet from his clipboard and handed it to Damon. "You're going to need this. Apparently, it's the groom's copy."

Damon flipped through a manifesto of the wedding arrangements, which had been put together by Jenna's wedding planning company, Beaumonts, and which emanated the same light floral fragrance as the pamphlet. The elaborate schedule included prewedding drinks and canapés, a session with a photographer, then a wedding dinner. *As if the marriage was real.*

It went without saying that it was totally at odds with Damon's plans, which consisted of briefly worded vows and signed and witnessed contracts, all completed in the space of twenty minutes in Hennessey's office.

Flipping open his briefcase, he dropped the manifesto on top of the thick sheaf of contracts and business papers he'd brought to peruse that evening—*his wedding night*—and closed the case with a controlled click.

A little grimly, he noted that, when he had decided on Chloe as his convenient bride, he had fully expected that the deal would decisively end his long-running, lingering relationship with Jenna. Most women would have walked away, but Jenna had done the exact opposite—she had crashed his wedding. "Is she here?"

Hennessey frowned. "Chloe?"

For a moment, Damon had actually forgotten about his bride-to-be. "Jenna."

"Oh, *her*. Uh—she was here last night and this morning with a team of florists and interior decorators—"

"Those would be the ninjas," Caleb murmured.

Hennessey's expression didn't change, but the temperature in the room dropped by a couple of degrees, reminding Damon that, as easygoing as Hennessey usually was, he was ex-army and had done two tours of Afghanistan before calling it quits.

Hennessey fixed Caleb with a steady look. "They

were dressed in black and carrying out the hunting trophies. It looked like a crime in progress."

Privately, Damon thought the real crime had happened in this room, but he kept that thought to himself.

Hennessey transferred his attention back to Damon. "Once they finished with the bridal suite, everyone left—except Ms. Beaumont."

Which meant Jenna was here for the wedding.

So much for trying to exclude her from his life.

His head came up as something else registered. "What bridal suite?"

Hennessey gave him the kind of look that suggested he was still trying to answer the same question. "I told Ms. Beaumont that you had already booked separate accommodations for Chloe, but she said that the bride had, uh—*insisted* on the cabin that overlooks the valley, because it's more private…and has a king-size bed and a spa."

Caleb said something short and flat. "I knew it. You should have looked for someone older and more reliable. Chloe's about as consistent as a butterfly."

Damon's jaw tightened. If he didn't miss his guess, she had been swayed by the online hype that had turned him from a reclusive bachelor into the Houston Stallion, because it now looked like she was trying to turn this marriage into the real thing.

He guessed he should have foreseen this particular pitfall since, within days of inheriting Alan Wyatt's billions a year ago, he had gone from the cowboy and roughneck no one wanted their daughter to date to Texas's most eligible bachelor.

Caleb, who had his phone out and was flicking through screens, muttered, "So, when, exactly is the bride supposed to arrive?"

Damon checked his watch. It was almost ten. Thanks to Chloe's frustrating excuses and delays, which had included a holiday in the Bahamas that she had already booked, their wedding date had been pushed a full week past the original scheduled date. As it stood, the wedding was supposed to take place around four that afternoon, leaving just an eight-hour cushion before his deadline ran out at midnight. "She should be here now. Ransom's not that far away."

There was a small silence. "What if she has to fly in from Houston? Today?"

Arrested by the odd flatness of Caleb's tone, Damon dragged his gaze from a large silver stand next to the cupcakes, which he was pretty sure was designed to hold a wedding cake. "What makes you think she's doing that?"

She lived in Houston and had an apartment about a fifteen-minute drive from his River Oaks mansion, but she had assured him she would spend last night at her family's holiday home in Ransom.

Caleb turned the screen of his phone so that Damon could see a snapshot of Chloe, surrounded by a be-sequined crush of female friends as she took a selfie at what looked like a nightclub. Damon noted the garish pink print across the base of the picture: Girls' Night Out.

A bachelorette party.

"Well, at least that answers that question," he said bleakly.

Although the fact that Chloe was in Houston last night, when she should have been in Ransom, faded when he noticed what she was wearing. The silky blue dress, almost identical to one that Jenna owned, spun him back three months, to the night he had rescued her from her dinner-date-gone-wrong and, out of the blue, desire hummed through him.

A little grimly, he noted that, aside from not foreseeing that in contracting Chloe to marry him, he would end up with Jenna as a wedding planner, he had made another tactical error.

Physically, Jenna and Chloe were chalk and cheese. Jenna was athletic with a faintly imperious nose, long, sleek hair and a classic style, while Chloe had cute features, razor-cut blond hair, a love of bright clothes and a number of zany tattoos and body piercings.

What was the same, and what kept shunting him back into the past with Jenna, were the personality traits—the high-maintenance lifestyle that went with the pampered, diamond-encrusted worlds they had been born into and the take-no-prisoners directness.

Too late to realize that, in making the decision to marry Chloe, he had opened a Pandora's box, because the second he had found out that Jenna had become entangled with the wedding, the heated, addictive desire he had done his level best to forget over the last month had flared to aching life.

To make matters worse, instead of being annoyed that his strategy had backfired, a renegade part of him was fiercely glad that it had.

Because, despite everything, he still wanted Jenna Beaumont back in his bed.

Damon Wyatt was getting married.

High-end wedding planner Jenna Beaumont paused in the act of scooping bespoke, handmade rose petals from a wooden box, which she had bought with her for the express purpose of sprinkling through the bridal chamber. Although, somehow, the delicate white silk petals just didn't go with the rustic setting of Pleasant River Lodge. Plus, every time she thought about her dark and dangerous ex, her mind did a weird disconnect.

As turbulent as their painful, distant past had been, it was the recent two-month liaison—she hesitated to call it a relationship, because Damon had been absent more than he had been present—that was really making her see red. A Damon she was still having trouble reconciling because, dressed in designer suits and smelling of some tantalizing cologne, his dark gaze cool and level, he was a far cry from the remote and untamable bad boy she had once fallen for.

Taking a deep breath, she loosened off her grip on the rose petals, which she was crushing, and shoved them back into the box.

To put what could only be labeled as a third regrettable mistake with Damon in its best context, she had gotten confused. She had thought she was dealing with the old Damon—for argument's sake, let's call that Damon Jekyll—and that, finally, they might have reached a place where they were both ready to engage in a genuine, viable relationship.

Instead, she had made the horrible mistake of spending a number of disconnected nights, when Damon had been able to fit her into his very busy schedule, with the *new* Damon. The Damon who turned up after dark, received stock market alerts and had telephone conversations with brokers in London and New York that necessitated him leaving before dawn. And, you guessed it, in the dark, almost as if he didn't want to be seen leaving her apartment. A Damon whose code name was Hyde.

And, maybe, she should repeat the one-month-ago-time reference for their breakup. Four weeks was not a huge stretch of time, but Damon had packed a lot of living into it. Just *four days* after he'd left her, he had been seen *publicly* dating another woman, a situation that still annoyed her intensely, since he had only ever engaged in clandestine trysts with her. To add insult to injury, just over two weeks after that, he had gotten *engaged* to her cousin Chloe.

In a sane, ordered universe, how could that happen?

Answer? She had no clue, which was why, when Chloe had asked her to be her wedding planner—after the first jolt of fury had faded—she had thought about it for a whole five seconds before saying yes.

At that point neither hell nor high water would

have stopped her from attending the wedding in some capacity, because, if there was one thing she was certain of, it was that neither Damon nor Chloe could possibly be in love. At this point, step away from Jekyll and Hyde and think Hades and Persephone, or oil and water, because Damon and Chloe just didn't fit.

Chloe was sunny, popular and rich. To date, she had been happily speed dating her way through every eligible bachelor in Houston, doing what the women in their family had been doing for generations—focusing on finding Mr. Right.

Diving into a secret, instant marriage with Damon, who had a reputation for not committing, just didn't make sense.

Was she suspicious?

Was the moon landing real? Did Britney have blond hair?

Of course she was suspicious. Especially since, aside from the nights he had spent with her, she had found that Damon had been dating up a storm, not just before he got engaged to Chloe, but *after*, and she had the evidence to prove it.

Which was one of the reasons, aside from the hefty fee Chloe had insisted she take for organizing the wedding—and which, by the way, she desperately needed—that she was making it her business to see for herself whether or not Damon was for real.

If he wasn't, well…just watch this space. In the South, family mattered, and it was a fact that Chloe was the closest thing she had to a sister. And since

Chloe's parents were both overseas, the way Jenna saw it, it was up to her to give Chloe the wedding of her dreams. *And* to find out exactly why a man who had vowed that he would never marry was suddenly marrying her cousin.

As always, the thought sent a weird jolt through her. She knew she shouldn't compare her own experiences with Damon, but a tiny part of her couldn't help thinking that her cousin had dated Damon for sixteen days, max, then most of the last week she had been away on vacation in the Bahamas. It was hardly the behavior of a bride preparing to marry the love of her life.

Sixteen days and Chloe had gotten a proposal.

Jenna had slept with Damon for *two months* and had gotten…nothing.

A flash of Damon, the morning after the last night they had slept together, increased the tension that had been steadily growing during the last twenty-four hours as she had overseen the setting up of the wedding venue, sending a confusing flood of emotions and a disturbing heat zinging through her.

A month ago, she had awoken in the early hours to find Damon propped on his side, watching her, sleek broad shoulders limned by the moonlight that flowed through the French doors that opened out onto her small patio. She had reached up to cup his roughened jaw, trace the softness of his lips and draw him down to her. But, instead of taking the kiss, he had held back, lacing his fingers with hers, and, for a startling moment, she had gotten the distinct impression that he was going to ask her something—something important. Maybe, even, that he had finally realized that they were good together and that he wanted a real relationship after all.

Out of nowhere her heart had begun to pound and her stomach had dropped as if she had just stepped to the edge of a precipice she hadn't known was there. She was twenty-eight and it had been six years since they had last been together in such an intimate way and she had *missed* Damon, missed this.

Then his phone had vibrated and the moment had gone. He had climbed from her bed to take what was obviously a business call from another time zone. Picking up his clothes as he talked, he had strolled naked to the shower. Fifteen minutes later, he had emerged, six feet two inches of lean, muscular male, damp and shirtless.

Another call on his phone, a check of the time on his watch, then he had finished dressing, leaned over and kissed her briefly on the mouth before telling her that he had to leave because he had an early flight...

Jenna closed the lid of the wooden box that held the rose petals with a snap.

The romantic, floral touch definitely didn't go with the heavy architecture of the cabin, the gray and oatmeal bed coverings, heavy wooden floors and cowhide rug, *or* the intimidating set of antlers sprouting from the wall opposite the bed.

Returning the box to her tote, she extracted a goody bag of handmade chocolates imprinted with the elegant logo of Beaumonts which also happened to be an old family crest on her mother's side.

But when she attempted to place the gorgeous, individually wrapped pralines on the pillows of the king-size bed, that also proved difficult, because she *knew* which side Damon would choose. Just looking at the pristine white pillow brought back a raft of memories. Among them, the unsettling fact that, while she'd always had a great deal of trouble letting go of what could only be considered a fatal attraction, Damon had had no such qualms. He had brought all three of their liaisons—the first, a totally unsatisfactory one-night stand; the second, a summer fling, which she had begun to believe was heading into real relationship territory; and the third, another totally unsatisfactory fling—to an end with a decisiveness that had stunned her.

Aka, he had ditched her. Three times.

In the history of the Montagues—that was her mother's side of the family—getting dumped, or even friend-zoned, was almost unheard-of. And, just to be clear, her mother was a New Orleans Montague. They were all killer good-looking with piercing blue eyes, cheekbones to die for, straight noses and firm chins. They were so perfect, it was almost as if they'd landed from another planet.

She hadn't—she had been born right here in Ransom—but she had inherited her mother's good looks. Add in a tan and combine that with the toned body that had gone with her cheerleading background and gym addiction, and she had been batting men off like flies for years.

All except for Damon.

When he pinned her with his dark blue gaze, her normally razor-sharp brain switched off, her hormones switched on and she ended up in bed with him. And it happened *fast*. The only thing she could liken it to was one of those blackout shopping experiences, when you end up out on the pavement with a maxed-out credit card, clutching a handful of designer bags, wondering what just happened.

With a brisk movement, she returned the pralines to the goody bag. After remembering the blunt way Damon had ditched her a month ago—*with a phone call*—giving one to him now felt a little too much like rewarding his bad behavior with chocolate.

Picking up a scented candle and the white linen his-and-hers robes that were one of her signature touches, she carried them through to the stylish but bleak gray bathroom. Dumping the perfectly folded robes on one end of the vanity, she set the candle down on the granite vanity top with a sharp click.

A quick inspection revealed that the expensive crystal container hadn't cracked, which was a relief, because she couldn't afford silly breakages. As successful as her business was, she wasn't exactly swimming in cash. Despite her soaring popularity as a wedding planner, lately she was crazy in the red thanks to the financial sinkhole the family law firm had become after her father's death. Add in the sky-high cost of paying Harvard fees for her younger brother, Luke, and she was close to bankruptcy. If she didn't find an immediate solution to her financial woes, both Beaumont Law and her wedding business would go belly-up.

Returning to the large studio bedroom, she glanced at the view over the extensive, smooth lawn that swept down to the Pleasant River. The distant hills with their dark blanketing of pines were barely visible, courtesy of thick storm clouds, steady, driving rain and a thick, creepy fog.

It was definitely *not* wedding weather. In fact, the weather app on her phone was calling it the edge of a category-two hurricane that was tracking in off the Gulf of Mexico. But then, nothing about this secretive, hurried wedding had a celebratory feel to it. Even Chloe, as insistent as she had been to have all the luxury touches, didn't seem bothered with the details. Her only instruction had been that Jenna should create the small, intimate wedding of *her* dreams, which was a worrying sign.

She understood that Chloe didn't have much time to get organized, but what bride wasn't interested in choosing her own cake or in poring over the details of the flower arrangements? Also, to her knowledge, there were no guests—Jenna was the only family member invited, and only because she was the wedding planner.

And Chloe didn't have a ring.

The lack of a ring was a clincher for Jenna, because it was a well-known fact that a man was at his most generous when he was courting. If a woman didn't receive the gift of an engagement ring, then she could cross love and appreciation off her list of future relationship expectations.

And Chloe *loved* diamonds. Like Jenna, she had been a debutante, and her parents and past boyfriends had showered her with some serious investment pieces to mark every possible occasion. If Chloe had accepted a marriage proposal without a serious rock on her finger, then Jenna's question was, who had stolen the real Chloe?

But the true kicker was that Chloe was *paying* for the wedding, clearly because she wanted to turn Damon's budget ceremony into something she might actually want to remember.

With brisk movements, Jenna straightened the plain array of bed cushions. It went without saying that she intended to get to the bottom of why her cousin was paying when Damon could buy and sell them all a hundred times over.

Jenna frowned at the emotions that kept surfacing—emotions she kept suppressing and didn't want to acknowledge, because they had no place in her role as a wedding planner.

Anger, betrayal and, unpalatably, *hurt* because, just when she had thought she and Damon were on the brink of something special, for reasons she couldn't fathom, he had walked away, then chosen Chloe over *her*.

It registered with a curious clarity that, in a few hours, he would be married to Chloe, that it would be Chloe in his bed.

Chloe, her cute, younger cousin who had followed her around, copying her clothes and makeup as a teenager, borrowing her shoes. Wanting to be her.

Chloe, now all grown up—*and stealing her guy*.

Jenna frowned at the thought.

That didn't make any kind of sense. Unless she had done something weird like repress old emotions and fail to get closure, which might explain the crawling tension that had gripped her the second Chloe had done her big reveal on her secret fiancé.

Her jaw set as she automatically vetoed that last thought. No way was she jealous.

That wasn't possible, because she was *over* Damon.

Two

Jenna did a perfunctory check that her assistant had filled the fridge with vintage champagne and a range of expensive cheeses and snacks, then gave the room a quick waft of her Beaumonts room spray before closing the door with a sharp click.

Before stepping out of the shelter afforded by the cabin's porch, she flipped up her umbrella, although it was scant protection in the wind and driving rain. By the time she had walked along the tree-lined path to the main building, her working uniform—a gorgeous blue Chanel suit that matched her eyes and that had a fitted little jacket and a short skirt that showed off possibly her best feature, her legs—was spotted with rain. Added to that her strappy blue heels were damp and plastered with small wet leaves, and her hair, which had started out as a neat coil, had loosened and strands were blowing around her face.

After reaching the nearest entrance into the sprawling, ultramodern lodge, she shook out her umbrella and left it at the side door while she went in search of the nearest ladies' room. A quick check of her watch made her stomach tense. When she'd run into the guy who ran the lodge, Hennessey, he had informed her that Damon should be here by midmorning, which was *now*.

Pushing open the restroom door, she paused before a large mirror and did a quick check of her appearance. She hadn't seen Damon since he had left her apartment a month ago, so no way was she going to meet him *on his wedding day* looking like she'd been dragged backward through a hedge.

Thankfully, her makeup was okay, and the diamond Chanel studs she had gotten as a gift from her parents when she graduated added a touch of class, but her hair was definitely wild.

Retrieving a comb from her tote, she smoothed her hair and wound it into a loose, sexy knot before repinning it. After cleaning the leaves off her shoes, she reapplied gloss to her lips then headed in the direction of the reception room she had chosen for the wedding ceremony. Aside from confronting Damon with her concerns, she needed to do one final check before she drove into Ransom and picked up Chloe's wedding cake and dress, which had been express delivered that morning.

Bare yards from the reception room, the low tim-bre of male voices made her tense.

Taking a deep breath, she strolled into the room. Damon was easy to spot. Inches taller than the other two men in the room, with broad shoulders, dark sable hair that brushed the collar of his very expensive suit and a rock-solid jaw, he looked like he would be more at home wielding a broadsword than a calculator. Although Jenna was well aware that a soulless calculator was more Damon's style these days, because, according to a long list of women who had dated him then been discarded—including herself—it had replaced his heart.

His head turned, his dark gaze clashed with hers and she was instantly aware of two things. First of all, he'd known she was here, so she had lost her element of surprise.

Second, there was an unexpected flare of awareness in his gaze, which threw her off balance, sent adrenaline zinging through her veins and made *her* all too aware of him. That was totally unacceptable when Damon was about to marry her cousin.

Flushing guiltily, and doing her level best to nix the inappropriate tension, she came to a halt barely a yard from the small group of men.

Hennessey, whom she'd had a few tense words with earlier because he had actually thought she was trying to get her hands on his dusty hunting trophies, made gruff introductions.

Although she had only met him in passing, she was familiar enough with Caleb, a high-flying lawyer, whom Chloe had dated for a few weeks. She just hadn't realized that he worked for Damon. But at least that connected the dots around how Damon had met her cousin.

Damon's gaze touched on hers again, sending another one of those unnerving little jolts through her. "We need to talk."

Jenna countered his cool, curt tone with a smooth, professional smile. "Perhaps later. First I need to check with the chef that he's up to speed with the canapés. Apparently, he was having trouble getting the beluga caviar in Ransom. Then I'm driving into town—"

"We need to talk. *Now.*"

Damon's hand closed around her elbow. The brief contact sent a sharp electrical tingle through her as she found herself turned around and urged in the direction of the far corner of the room.

Jerking free from his grip, she marched the last few yards to the flowery arch, which seemed to be the destination he was aiming for, but she was only cooperating because she was aware that, if the gloves were coming off, they were going to need a little privacy for what *she* had to say.

Hitching the strap of her tote more firmly over her shoulder, she made a production of checking the time. She wasn't in a hurry yet, but it didn't hurt Damon to know that she was busy. "Okay," she said smoothly. "What, exactly, did you want to say?"

He gave her a long, considering look, as if he was fast losing his patience. In other circumstances,

Jenna might have considered that look sexy and just a little edgy, but right now, it went under the label of controlling.

"Why are you here?"

Even though she was braced for a reaction, Damon's softly worded question was unexpectedly hurtful.

Her chin came up. "I could ask you the same question, because, until Chloe sprang the news on me a week ago that she was getting married to you, I didn't even know the two of you had met."

He crossed his arms over his chest. "Okay, I'll play. I've known your cousin for a while, ever since she was dating Caleb."

She drew a deep breath and asked the question she didn't want to ask, and which she didn't want to be important, but which was because she had *slept* with him. And she didn't sleep with just anyone. In fact, she had only ever slept with Damon, which meant something. In a life filled with handsome, eligible guys, from whom she could pick and choose—and regularly did—it was an irritating statistic. Although not as irritating as the fact that Damon himself had never realized that she had been a virgin the first time they had slept together.

She guessed that, at age nineteen, she had thought he would *know*, but the fact that he had never exhibited any curiosity about whether she had been a virgin or not was somehow symptomatic of everything that had gone wrong with them. "Were you interested in Chloe when we were…together?"

"Not at that point, no."

"But you started dating her not long after we broke up." Swallowing to try and smooth out the sudden huskiness of her voice, she stared at the pulse beating along the side of his jaw. "Why didn't you *say* something?"

And why had he slept with her if he had really wanted to be with Chloe?

His gaze was shuttered. "Because I hadn't made any decisions at that point."

Not the right answer.

"But you clearly did make some kind of a decision when you closed the door on our—relationship." Even using that word made her mad, because it was increasingly clear that, at no point, had he ever wanted more from her than sex.

There was a small, tense silence during which she became aware that, at some point, Hennessey and Caleb, thankfully, had left the room.

"I'm sorry if I hurt you—"

"*Surprised* is a better word," she said crisply. Although that was an outright lie, because when Chloe had called to tell her that she and Damon were marrying in a few days' time, for long moments she had been, literally, paralyzed by shock and hurt.

Shock because, even though Damon had left her and had dated someone else, she had been silly enough to actually think he might decide he'd made a mistake and give her a call. Hurt because she had thought that their lovemaking had had a different quality to it, that there was something different about

Damon, a softness and an openness that had signaled that some time in the future, they might actually have a chance at the real relationship she had wanted.

His gaze was remote. "My decision had nothing to do with the fact that you and I slept together."

She plastered a professional smile on her face. "I guess what I want to know," she said coolly, "is, how you can sleep with someone for two months then decide to marry someone else a couple of weeks later?"

He frowned. "We didn't sleep together the whole two months—"

"No, because you were away a lot. But we did share a bed when you were in Houston. According to my diary, that was *nineteen* nights."

"Like I said, I'm sorry if I hurt you."

Damon might be sorry, but she was still confused. Jenna had never heard Chloe so much as mention Damon as a guy she thought was hot and attractive. The clincher was that her cousin knew that Damon was Jenna's ex.

In terms of the girl code alone, Damon should be off-limits to Chloe. Which probably explained why she had broken the news over the phone, listened to Jenna's concern that she wasn't ready to cope with the toughness and walls that came from Damon's past, then had disappeared for a week's vacation!

Suddenly over Damon's sphinxlike answers, Jenna crossed her arms over her chest. "I guess that brings us to the only question that can have an answer, which is, what am *I* doing here?"

Damon frowned. "I think we've covered that question."

Heat flared in her cheeks that Damon clearly thought the only reason she was here was to make trouble. "No," we haven't," Jenna said flatly. "First of all, Chloe asked me to plan her wedding, knowing that, because we're family, it would be hard for me to refuse, despite my busy schedule. Secondly, I wanted to be here for my cousin, because she deserves to have at least *one* family member at her wedding—"

"Speaking of Chloe—" Damon glanced at his watch, which was just a little annoying, because now he was making her feel as if she was imposing upon his valuable time. "Do you know where she is?"

Jenna shot him a fiery glance. "Last I heard, she was booked to fly in from Houston this morning."

"She was supposed to be here, or in Ransom, last night."

And Chloe had clearly not followed orders.

Annoyed by his dictatorial tone and the fact that her heart was still pounding way too fast, Jenna met his gaze squarely. "I'm sure Chloe's not far away. If she's not with you already, it's probably because she's had a busy schedule—"

"Like the bachelorette party in Houston."

She took another deep breath and let it out slowly. "Last I heard it's not the Dark Ages. Bachelorette parties are allowed. I don't see what's wrong with Chloe enjoying her last night of freedom—"

"Before she gets shackled to me?"

Jenna plowed on, ignoring the interruption. "Men

have bachelor parties to celebrate their loss of freedom." A freedom Damon had been enjoying before and after his engagement, if social media reports were to be believed. "Why shouldn't women have the same privilege?"

He pinched his nose, which was beyond infuriating. "I didn't have a bachelor party," he said flatly. "My whole point is that Chloe knew she was supposed to be here."

"It's not my fault you can't find your fiancée," she said crisply. "I'm just the wedding planner. If you're having trouble getting hold of Chloe, it's probably because she's on her flight, or the cell coverage out here is so bad. *Or* she's gotten lost, because, quite frankly, you need a map to find this place."

"You and your team of florists didn't seem to have any trouble finding it."

"It's the twenty-first century…we have GPS."

"Which brings me to the next question." Damon jerked his head at the wedding table and the arch. "Whose idea was all of this?"

Jenna's fingers tightened on her tote. She also noticed that one toe was tapping on the floor, a small habit she had inherited from her mother, and which was a *sign*, because Catherine Beaumont had had a terminally short fuse when it came to organizational matters, and Jenna was a chip off her mother's starched linen shoulder. "I don't even know why you're asking that. Hell would freeze solid before I'd offer my services. It was all Chloe's idea, but I'm guessing from your question it wasn't yours."

"Not exactly."

"Hence the hunting lodge, and the fact that it's Chloe who's paying the bills."

There was a small, vibrating silence. "The agreement was that she didn't organize, or pay for, anything," he said bleakly. "The ceremony was supposed to take place in Hennessey's office, and the lodge was chosen because it belongs to me, which means the media doesn't have access."

A secret office wedding.

Jenna and Chloe's shared great-grandmother, Eugenie Montague, who had owned a wedding empire in New York, would spin in her grave.

But what really irked Jenna was that Damon was trying to hide the wedding. She had thought the secrecy thing only applied to her, but clearly he had a serious issue around being open about any relationship. "You want to keep the marriage…a secret?"

"Putting my private life online isn't exactly a focus."

Jenna's cheeks warmed at the deliberate reference to her feeding the details of their "top-secret" liaison to Chantal Sanderson, a blogger who had a reputation for exposing juicy gossip to huge audiences.

In an ideal world, she wouldn't have behaved that way, but when she had found out that he had been organizing to date some woman she had never heard of literally hours after he left her bed, she had lost it. That unknown woman had gotten a *date*, something that Damon had neglected to do for her, so she refused to apologize for putting it out there that they had been having an actual relationship.

A little grimly, she noted that Damon clearly *had* wanted to keep his marriage to Chloe quiet. What was his problem?

"What about Chloe?" she demanded. "What if she expects just a little more from you than a utilitarian, hole-in-the-corner affair?"

But, suddenly, for Jenna, it wasn't about Chloe at all—it was about Damon's utter lack of consideration for her, and the fact that he had been more than happy to keep their relationship under wraps on *three* separate occasions.

It all added up to Damon having zero interest in claiming her as his, except for one notable occasion. That had been six years ago, when she had forced the issue by deliberately walking arm in arm on the main street of Ransom with Brad Henderson, a lawyer her parents had been pressuring her to date, when she knew Damon would be in town.

But, as dizzying as the moment had been when Damon strode into battle for her and confronted Brad, even that had backfired, because it had precipitated their breakup. Like their recent liaison, she'd been left with the indelible impression that for Damon, when it came to her, the whole idea of a relationship was nonexistent, because all they truly shared was sex.

His expression was remote. "Chloe knew exactly what she agreed to. Until I got here half an hour ago, I thought we were on the same page. And," he stated bleakly, "if we'd needed a wedding venue and a wedding planner, I can assure you, I would have paid for it."

And suddenly they were close enough that she could smell the fresh scent of soap and a whiff of some expensive cologne, feel the heat emanating from Damon's big body. Her chin came up, which was a necessity because he was a good eight inches taller than her. The only problem with that was that she got entangled in the net of his gaze.

"Look," Damon said in a curt, deep voice, "about the marriage to Chloe —"

A burst of soothing classical music signaled that Jenna had a call. Relieved to break the stifling awareness that had, once again, crept up on her, she extracted the phone from her bag, checked the screen and saw Brad's name.

She frowned. After not seeing much of Brad for years, she'd had a business meeting with him just a few days ago in the hope that he would buy in to Beaumont Law. Frustratingly, he had gone to Los Angeles and she hadn't expected to hear from him until he returned in a few weeks' time. But, whatever he was calling about, it occurred to her that his timing couldn't be better.

"Brad," she said brightly, slanting Damon a semi-apologetic look as she held the phone to her ear and strolled a few steps away.

The call was short. Apparently, during their business dinner, she had introduced Brad to an old crony of her father's, a former senator, and now he wanted his number. She didn't have it, which brought the conversation to an abrupt end. Frowning, because normally Brad was smooth and charming, she turned back to Damon, who was now staring broodingly out at the drenched landscape.

His gaze pinned hers. "I take it that was Brad Henderson. If you'll take my advice, you should step back from him—"

"Luckily for me, I don't need your advice," she pointed out firmly. For a start, she had never felt the remotest attraction to Brad, so it was hardly likely they would ever be close that way. Added to that, Damon might be a ranching and oil billionaire, but he was definitely no love doctor.

She checked her Fitbit, which, aside from registering a crazy-high heartbeat, told her that it was past time she left. "I'm glad we had this little chat," she said smoothly, "but, right now I need to drive into Ransom and pick up on some final details for your wedding. After all, I wouldn't want there to be any hitches at this point. Not now that you've finally decided to commit to *someone*."

Three

Damon walked into the suite he would be using while he was at the lodge.

Jenna still wanted him.

In the midst of a conversation that had been peppered with a number of revelations, including the fact that, evidently, he was still living in the Dark Ages, that was the one singular piece of knowledge that had riveted him to the spot as he had watched Jenna drive away from the lodge in a silver SUV.

It was also the last thing he wanted to learn when he was on the verge of a marriage of convenience to another woman, because the reason he had counted Jenna out of marriage hadn't changed. He couldn't afford her in his life because he still wanted her, and that one salient fact opened him up to the world of hurt he'd seen played out between his parents, and which he was determined to avoid.

His first encounter with her had been a case in point. Ten years ago, during his senior year at Houston University, when he'd played quarterback for the Cougars, Jenna, who had been new on the cheerleading squad, had walked onto the practice field. Slim and gorgeous in pink Lycra, she had smiled and winked at him, and he'd been a goner.

Two days later, after they had slept together, she had told her father that she was planning on seeing him and he'd gotten a call from Henry Beaumont, who had made it explicitly clear that his daughter was off-limits. Damon was inclined to agree, since Jenna was the kind of woman he had long ago sworn off: an assured Southern debutante who was even more privileged and pampered than his mother had been.

He had backed off, but six years ago, when he'd rescued Jenna on one of Ransom's back roads after her sports car had broken down, the attraction had gotten out of hand again, and he had kissed her. If she had rebuffed him, he would have apologized and walked away. Instead, Jenna had curled her fingers into the lapels of his shirt and kissed him back.

After years of keeping his distance, he hadn't been able to resist, but in an effort to put the brakes on, he had made it clear he hadn't wanted more than one night. Two months later, they had still been embroiled in the kind of addictive, steamy liaison he hadn't been able to end, a liaison he had insisted they keep under wraps until he had driven into town one day and seen Jenna walking down Main Street, arm in arm with Brad Henderson.

Ignoring the car behind him, Damon had jammed on the brakes and double-parked. At that point he had realized two things. Firstly, that despite his determination to see their time together as temporary and just about no-strings sex, at some point he had crossed a line. They came from two different worlds, and Jenna's family didn't want him anywhere near her, but, despite that, and his own reservations, he had wanted to tie Jenna to him.

Secondly, seeing Jenna with Brad had made him realize that there was more at stake for her in agreeing to keep their relationship quiet than simply overprotective parents and town gossip. He didn't want to think that Jenna had agreed to the secrecy because all along she had been planning on marrying Henderson, but he would have to have been brain-dead to miss the clues.

A knock on the door distracted Damon as he checked his phone again. There was still no sign of a call or text from Chloe and, frustratingly, when he tried to call, there was no reply. Although if she was on a flight, her phone would be on airplane mode.

He opened the door. Caleb stepped in, carrying his briefcase. "I've got the final draft of the marriage contract. You'd better take a look at it before Chloe gets here." Dropping his briefcase on a coffee table, he flipped it open. "Still can't get my head around the fact that you actually have to get married."

Neither could Damon.

After the car crash his parents' marriage had been, it had been a no-brainer to swear off marriage altogether. Unfortunately, Alan Wyatt hadn't seen it that way.

A grim snapshot of his once pretty socialite mother and his father, Cole Wyatt—a ranch hand who had devolved into a brawler and a drunk—tearing the house apart with their fighting was still vivid enough to make his stomach hollow out.

At age twelve, when his mother had finally walked out, taking her trust fund and the deed of the house her family had paid for, she had left him behind. The reason? She claimed she couldn't take him with her to her parents' hillside mansion because, apparently, he looked just a little too much like Cole Wyatt and was a reminder of the mistake she had made in marrying a down-on-his-luck cowboy.

Weeks later, evicted from the nice neighborhood they had lived in, Damon and his father had ended up in a ramshackle cottage at the wrong end of town. At that point, life had gotten both better and worse. There were no more fights at home, but Cole's drinking, womanizing and public brawling had escalated. Damon had spent most of his teenage years dragging his father out of bars, breaking up fights and evicting a steady stream of casual lovers who emptied his father's wallet even faster than the bars.

Marriage? He would sooner be dragged backward through a herd of stampeding cattle.

Damon took the envelope and extracted the contract, which was in triplicate.

He systematically flicked through the pages. Caleb and his legal team had gone to a great deal of trouble to pick through the terms of the will and draw up a marriage agreement that exactly matched Alan Wyatt's requirements and Damon's own precise instructions.

The fact that the marriage required little more than a ceremony, a signed marriage contract and shared living for two months had made getting married acceptable. But, aware of his status as one of Houston's most eligible bachelors, and the online hype that had blatantly branded him as a stud, Damon had been determined to make it clear that sex was not on this particular menu. The detailed clauses, which extended to separate mealtimes, separate suites and scheduled bathroom times, were a little excessive. But after going a few rounds with Caleb, in the end they had run out of time, so Damon had reluctantly approved the document.

He dropped the envelope and the agreements onto the coffee table. "Good work, but it reads more like a set of barracks rules than a marriage agreement."

Caleb, who had walked through to the kitchen to put coffee on, carried two steaming mugs into the sitting room. "If you don't want to end up married for real, it needs to be." He set the mugs down on the coffee table. "Two months from now, you'll be free and clear." He frowned. "By the way, have you heard from Chloe?"

A heavy gust of wind hit the side of the lodge with enough force to make the cedar timbers creak, and the rain seemed to notch up another gear, pounding the floor-to-ceiling bifolds.

Damon checked his phone then hit the call button on her number again, without any luck. "She's still not answering. But if she's flying into Ransom, her phone's probably in airplane mode." He went online and found the flight times. Since there was only one last flight scheduled for the day, that had to be it. "Looks like she should be landing in a couple of hours."

Caleb walked to the window and stared at the now torrential rain as he drank a mouthful of coffee. "Has she been here before? This place is *isolated*."

"If the wedding planner and the florists found this place," Damon growled, "then Chloe can."

"I guess she should make it, then."

Damon joined Caleb at the window and stared at the once-shallow river that flowed around the lodge. In the space of the last half hour, it had deepened significantly.

Suddenly, the decision to have the wedding at the lodge—where he could keep it as low-key as possible—came back to haunt him. There was only one road in, but, in this weather, it would require four-wheel drive.

There was only one option. "Hennessey runs a four-wheel-drive cab service for guests. I'll ask him to pick her up from the airport."

Caleb's phone pinged, indicating that a text had

just come in. A few moments later, he said, "No need to bother Hennessey. I have to get a couple of things from town. I'll pick her up."

Jenna drove slowly on the return journey from Ransom, because the storm, which was supposed to have faded, had definitely worsened. Heavy rain poured down on a rough-hewn, lonely landscape, and the wind was gusting, sending leaves and small branches flying.

Luckily, she had brought her gorgeous, almost-new SUV, because she knew she'd have to pick up Chloe's dress and the cake, so she felt reasonably safe. The SUV had four-wheel drive. She had never had occasion to use it, but if she had to, that wasn't a problem, because she had grown up driving four-wheel-drive vehicles.

She slowed for a piece of road that had overflowing drains, then sped up again, her wipers working overtime. A quick check of her navigational system told her she wasn't that far from the lodge, and her stomach tightened in response.

She had done her level best to stay calm when she had confronted Damon. Unfortunately, it had been the first time she had seen him since he had ditched her a month ago, and she had lost it.

The problem was that she was so used to picking and choosing whom she dated, and being the one to say yes or no to a relationship, that having Damon shut the door in her face, again, had really ground her gears. He had even had the effrontery to tell her to stay away from Brad, as if he had every right to veto whom she dated!

Not that she was dating Brad. Their dealings were strictly business. Although, he had shocked her by casually letting it drop that he was still interested in a relationship with her, because, apparently, it was an advantage for his next career for him to be married.

Jenna had managed to keep a polite expression on her face because it was a fact that, six years ago, instead of settling for Brad as her parents had wanted her to do, she had run in the opposite direction— straight into Damon's arms.

But, as uninterested in Brad as she was, and despite his out-of-the blue comment about marriage, she *was* still hopeful that he would take up her offer to become a partner at Beaumont Law.

Jaw taut, she picked up her phone and dialed Brad's number. She hadn't been able to talk to him about the partnership proposal when he'd called earlier because Damon had been standing broodingly over her, but there was nothing stopping her from doing that now.

When Brad answered, his voice was faintly irritable and there was a lot of background noise. Apparently he was in a meeting of some kind.

The conversation was short and to the point. Brad had indicated a lukewarm interest in a partnership with Beaumont Law but, when she mentioned she was getting her lawyer to draft a proposal to run by him, he suddenly seemed on the verge of backing out.

Jenna had to keep reminding herself that he was a lawyer and ten years older than herself so, of course, he was naturally cautious. It was a characteristic she found mildly irritating but one that would make him perfect for a senior partnership.

Feeling just a little annoyed, she terminated the call.

Suddenly, no matter how desperate she was, it didn't seem like a good idea to entrust Beaumont Law to Brad. Although, her stomach hollowed out at the thought that she was going to have to start her search for a senior partner all over again.

She slowed in time to negotiate another piece of partially flooded road. Loosening her grip on the wheel, she continued on more cautiously.

As she approached the Pleasant River, which was just five minutes from the lodge, she noted that the water had risen significantly since she'd driven over it just two and a half hours ago. It now bore no resemblance to its name as it surged along like a freight train, murky with silt.

This close to the lodge, her thoughts instantly shifted back to the confrontation with Damon. But, as she drove down the long slope toward the bridge, she couldn't regret telling him what she thought of him. Jenna's fingers tightened on the wheel as, for a split second, the road ahead dissolved, to be replaced by a flash of Damon lying naked, sprawled in her bed in a tangle of white sheets, his jaw darkened by a five-o'clock shadow, his face softened by sleep…

A split second later, a large but innocent-looking

puddle that was unexpectedly deep sent water spraying up around the SUV and threw the vehicle into a weird, sideways slip.

Her foot automatically pumped the brake, but in the wet conditions the tires couldn't get a solid grip and she continued to slide and fishtail toward the bridge.

Leaving the brake alone, she concentrated on attempting to keep the SUV straight. She was just a few yards from the bridge and the swollen river when the rear clipped a road sign, sending the SUV skating sideways again. Moments later, thankfully by now almost in slow motion, the SUV left the road.

It flashed through her mind that the airbags could deploy. Her right arm flung up to protect her face, a kneejerk reaction she had learned the hard way when she'd had a small accident in Houston a year ago and ended up with a broken nose and two black eyes.

As the SUV lurched nose-down into an overflowing ditch, the airbags ballooned with a loud pop.

As they deflated, she drew an incredulous breath. She couldn't believe it; this time she had actually saved her nose.

But what she really couldn't get over was that she had crashed her gorgeous new SUV because she had been thinking about Damon naked.

Four

Wrinkling her nose at the smell of burning rubber, which came from the airbags, Jenna unlatched her seat belt. Aside from being a little shaken, she was extremely happy she'd escaped injury and that, aside from being stuck in a ditch, and the dent the rear had no doubt sustained, the SUV seemed relatively unscathed.

Her biggest problem now was that the SUV was stuck in a ditch just yards from the end of the bridge and the river, and the vehicle was lying at something close to a thirty-degree angle.

She pressed the starter button. Nothing happened. There were no lights, not even a flicker of life. Her console was blank, which confirmed that her electrics weren't working.

Her stomach sank. At some point, either when she'd driven through the puddle or when she'd gone into the ditch, water must have sprayed up into the engine and drenched the wiring. If that was the case, the SUV was out of commission and she was going to need a tow.

But before she rang the lodge to see if someone could come down and help her out, she needed to do all she could to ensure there wasn't another accident by making the silver SUV, which would be close to invisible in this misty weather, as visible as possible to oncoming traffic.

Unclipping her seat belt, she peeled away the remnants of the passenger-side airbag, opened the glove box and found the visibility vest and the small flashlight that were stored there. The plan was to wedge the flashlight between the wing mirror and the side of the SUV, then drape the vest over the trunk.

The only problem was, she couldn't open the electric windows. Duh.

That would be because they were electric.

Bracing herself for the weather, she opened the door. Wind and rain swirled around her as she stared down at the water lapping at her SUV. It was not a good moment to discover that most of the water in the ditch was actually river water, courtesy of the fact that the river was so high.

Not good. Also, her leather boots were crazy expensive. If she stepped into the ditch, they would be ruined. And it was a safe bet that if she *did* step into the ditch, which was super muddy, she would slide down and her jeans would also get wet. It would be cleaner and way more sensible to clamber out of the back of the SUV, onto the edge of the road.

Closing the door against the rain, she climbed into the rear passenger seat. Luckily, she was casually dressed for the drive into Ransom, in stretch jeans, a sweater and a practical pair of lace-up leather boots, so car gymnastics was a breeze.

Pulling down one of the rear seats, which was designed to lie flat to extend the trunk space, she dragged the box with the wedding dress into the main part of the cab, shoved it to one side to make space for herself, then crawled through to the rear door.

Siding the box that held the wedding cake farther to one side, she found the lever and pulled it. There was a satisfying clunk as the lock disengaged, and there was movement, but when she tried to push the door open, it wouldn't budge.

One glance at the damaged paneling, explained why. The door was definitely buckled.

Feeling increasingly annoyed—because she needed to get back to the lodge ASAP, finish setting up for the wedding and have some one-on-one time with Chloe just to make sure she really did want to marry Damon—she probed the small gap around the edges of the trunk door. There was about an inch of space, just enough to get her fingers through. She applied pressure, but still no dice. A fiercer shove netted her a stinging sensation.

Frowning, she checked out her finger, which

she had managed to cut on something. Clambering through to the front, she found a tissue, blotted her finger and applied pressure for a few seconds. Satisfied that the bleeding had stopped, she tossed the tissue into the small trash sack she kept in the console between the two front seats.

She tried the power button again, just for kicks. When that didn't work, she decided to give up on trying to make the SUV more visible to nonexistent oncoming traffic. The smart thing to do now was to call the lodge, *if* she had cell phone coverage. She found her phone, which had slid off the front seat and ended up on the floor. She was scrolling through her contacts when the screen lit up and a call came through.

It registered that she finally had cell phone coverage, despite the last few minutes, when everything that could go wrong had gone wrong.

Damon's name flashed up on the screen. A sharp pulse of adrenaline arrowed through her veins.

He was, literally, the last man on earth she wanted to speak to right now, but she couldn't afford not to take this call.

"Jenna?"

Taking a deep breath, she tried to sound breezy and casual, as if she hadn't made the rookie mistake of driving too fast through water and had ended up nose-down in a ditch with a raging torrent just yards away. "*Damon.* It's good to finally speak with—"

"Is Chloe with you?"

His flat demand made her stiffen.

For the past few minutes, she had been systematically trying to rescue herself from an *emergency*. She knew that Damon didn't know any of that, but still…

A thud, as if something had just hit the bridge pilings—probably a log that had been washed downstream—distracted Jenna from a conversation that was fast going sideways. "Why would Chloe be with me? Last I heard, she was supposed to be flying in and would get to the lodge this afternoon. But, as it happens, I'm glad you've called, because   "

She had to take another deep breath against a sudden hit of emotion that made her chest feel banded and tight. Reaction, she guessed, to the shock of having an accident, and the relief of human contact when she had begun to feel horribly isolated and alone. Sucking in another breath, she attempted to keep her voice smooth and professional, but when she spoke, her voice sounded thick and husky even to her own ears. "I've had—a small accident."

"What kind of an accident?" There was a taut silence. "Babe, are you okay?"

The shift in Damon's tone, his use of "babe," as if they were still intimately connected, made her go still inside. Until that point the conversation had been edgy and a little conflicted. But with his take-charge manner and that one word, something had shifted, and she was reminded of why she had fallen for him all those years ago.

Apart from the fact that he was gorgeous and hot, Damon was a no-holds-barred alpha guy. When she had needed rescuing, he always seemed to be there.

"I'm fine," she muttered. "And the SUV is, too,

basically. I don't need medical assistance—all I need is a tow. I drove into some water on the road, and the car aquaplaned and went sideways. My biggest problem is that now I'm stuck just a few yards from the bridge, and I can't start the SUV."

"Which bridge?"

"The Pleasant River Bridge, although, right now, nothing around here looks that pleasant."

There was another short, tense silence. "How long have you been there?"

"A few minutes."

"If you drove into water, then the electrics have probably gotten wet. Was there any sound when you tried to start the engine?"

"Nothing. It's completely dead."

"That means the fuse box got flooded." Damon said something terse and flat. "Stay calm, and stay on this call. I'll be there in five minutes."

Jenna stared at the screen of her phone, which was still glowing with Damon's name. The conversation was effectively over, but the sense of being linked with him was almost palpable. She could hear him walking, registered his voice as he spoke to someone briefly. There was the click of a door closing then a crunching sound, as if he was walking over gravel.

After the tumult of the past week and the shock of finding out that he was Chloe's bridegroom, it was an odd feeling to be connected with Damon in such an intimate way.

"Are you still there?"

The low timbre of Damon's tone made her fingers tighten on the phone and spun her back to the slow, sleepy conversations she used to have with him while she'd watched him dress in the early hours of the morning. "I haven't hung up."

She heard the rumble of a truck as he started it, the change in sound quality as his phone connected to the truck's audio. She felt a little unnerved—not because of her predicament, but because she would see Damon in just a few minutes and that, crazily, was making her pulse race.

She set the phone down on the seat. As she did so, a heavy gust of wind buffeted the SUV, and water from the river sprayed over the bridge railings and spattered her windshield. Craning around, she checked out the river, which seemed a little higher than it had looked just minutes ago.

Suddenly, the fact that she'd driven into a ditch was decidedly secondary to the fact that the water was rising fast.

Had she mentioned the tiny fact that she had a phobia about water? And she was talking calm, limpid water and friendly beach waves, not raging white water that could quite possibly overrun the bridge and sweep her SUV away.

The thought galvanized her. She didn't think the SUV would end up in the water, because the lodge was only a few minutes away, so Damon would get here before anything that dire could happen. But no way was she going to just sit here and wait for a rescue: she just wasn't that person. She needed to do something, like get the trunk open so it would be easy to unload the wedding cake and the dress.

Clambering back into the rear space, she had another go at trying to get the trunk to open, by using her feet to kick the door. Thanks to regular gym sessions and morning jogs, her legs were strong. Two kicks later and the door finally opened.

After snagging her stylish raincoat—which would be close to useless in this weather—she decided that, before she attempted to lift the wedding cake out of the SUV, she should check on it first.

The box that held the cake was still in approximately the same place, but the chances that it had survived the accident weren't good. A quick check revealed that the miniature bride and groom were half-buried in collapsed layers of vanilla cake, raspberries and buttercream. The designer cake, which had once been covered in delicate white scrollwork, was now a very messy disaster.

Feeling a distinct lack of emotion for the cake, which she had recently listed as her favorite cake on her wedding blog, she closed the box lid. It wasn't worth rescuing. Instead, she reached for the wedding dress. A quick check reassured her that at least the Vera Wang had survived without damage, but when her gaze fell on the tag attached to the dress, she said a bad word.

Chloe was tiny, and wore a size-two dress, but the dress was a four, which was Jenna's size.

"What's going on?"

The gravelly curtness of Damon's voice, preternaturally loud in the enclosed space of the SUV, almost making her jump out of her skin. She'd been so busy she had almost forgotten he was still on the call.

"The dress is the wrong size."

His muttered expletive was cut short by another massive gust of wind.

Seconds later, the glow of headlights cut through the gloom. Jenna used her sleeve to clean the condensation that had misted the side window and, out of nowhere, her heart squeezed tight. After the turmoil of the last few days, she never thought she'd be so pleased to see Damon.

A split second later, a muscular black truck braked to a halt just yards from the SUV, and her heart began to hammer. As she watched him climb out of his truck, his hair dripping, shirt soaked and clinging to his broad shoulders, because he clearly hadn't stopped to grab any-wet weather gear, it occurred to her that she couldn't wish for a better rescuer.

Damon's gaze connected with hers, and a hard jolt of awareness froze her in place. That was quickly replaced by a surge of panic and guilt, because he was Chloe's groom, not hers. Feeling anything except an efficient need to organize him into doing his part to make the wedding run like clockwork was just flat out wrong.

Suddenly crazy on edge, she closed the box that held the wedding dress.

The cake was a goner, but there was no way on this earth she was leaving the Vera Wang dress behind.

Five

Jaw tight, Damon pulled up near the SUV, which was nose-down in the ditch.

A little grimly, he noted that Jenna had given him the distinct impression that she had driven through water on the road and had gotten stuck. She hadn't mentioned that she was in a ditch just yards from a flooding river that was close to overrunning the bridge, *or* that she'd hit something.

When he'd driven down the hill, he had gotten a good look at the damage to the rear of the SUV, and the tension that had gripped him when Jenna had told him she'd had an accident ratcheted up another notch.

Just minutes ago, he'd been focused on the wedding and the fact that despite Caleb going to get Chloe, they had now both disappeared off the radar and neither were answering his calls. But the second he had understood Jenna was in danger, everything had changed.

Moments later, she stepped out into the water that pooled on the road, looking as if she'd just returned from a shopping expedition, with a stylish raincoat belted at her waist and a handbag looped over one shoulder.

Her gaze, which seemed dark against the pallor of her cheeks, locked with his, and his chest banded tight.

Part of him wanted to haul her close and hug her, and a part of him wanted to chew her out for leaving it until the end of their telephone conversation to tell him that she was in danger.

She dragged a long, narrow box from the buckled rear of the SUV.

"Leave the box," he said tersely.

"No."

"What could be that important?"

"A wedding dress. For your bride."

If he had thought she didn't care about the fact that he was getting married, he would have been wrong. Jenna's cool, assessing gaze practically cut him in two and, out of nowhere, his heart rate increased for a whole different reason than a life-threatening flood.

Feeling like he was picking up an exploding bomb, Damon took the box and deposited it into the rear seat of the double-cab truck. When he turned back, frustratingly, Jenna was once more back in the SUV. With the rising river close to swamping the vehicle, it was all he could do to keep his temper in check. She clambered out moments later, her phone in her hand.

Damon grabbed the winch rope attached to the front of Hennessey's truck. He had already positioned the truck so he could tow the SUV back up the slope. With the water still rising and the bridge on the verge of flooding, the SUV had to be moved to a safer place.

A spray of water exploded over the railings, soaking him anew as he quickly attached the rope to the tow hook just underneath the rear bumper of the SUV.

When he straightened, Jenna was still in exactly the same place he had seen her last, staring at the water that was now beginning to run across the surface of the bridge.

"What's wrong?" But, from the starkness of her expression, he guessed it before she said it.

"I'm not a fan of water."

Damon would have laid money on Jenna not being afraid of anything.

"Then don't look at it." Before he could stop himself, he stooped and swung her off her feet, into his arms. Her nose landed against his neck; the coldness of it and the warmth of her breath on his throat sent an unexpected wave of warmth surging through him.

Her arms automatically clamped around his neck. "I *can* walk."

His dark gaze clashed with hers. "For once, don't argue."

Damon set Jenna down beside the passenger side of the truck and opened the door for her. He waited, shielding her from the worst of the wind and rain, as she climbed into the passenger seat. By the time she had belted herself in, Damon had swung into the driver's side of the truck. As he pulled the door closed, the cessation of noise, and the pressure of the wind and rain, made the interior of the cab seem oddly intimate.

Clamping down on the all too familiar hum of awareness, he started the truck and began winching the SUV out of the ditch. Once it was clear, he backed up the hill, until the SUV was both off the road and well clear of the river. Braking, he disconnected the winch, reeled it in then drove them slowly across the bridge. When they reached the other side, he parked and turned, his gaze sweeping over Jenna. Despite the fact that her hair was wet and her skin was too pale, she looked, if possible, even more gorgeous.

"Please tell me you didn't see the water on the road before you drove over it."

"If I had," she said flatly, "I would have gone a lot slower and not had an accident."

"You could have been killed."

The words briefly flung him back to an incident he had almost forgotten—when he had taken her riding and she had climbed off her horse and almost stepped on a rattlesnake. Damon could still remember the cold panic that had gripped him as he had calmly talked her through it, telling her to freeze, to not move a muscle. They had both stood like statues in the blazing heat of the afternoon sun until the snake had finally slithered away. At that point, he had jerked her into his arms and given her a blistering telling off for dismounting before checking the ground. As much as he'd tried to keep his emotional distance, the thought that Jenna could have been hurt, or killed, had shaken him.

His gaze dropped to her hand. "Damn, you've hurt yourself."

She glanced at her finger, which was oozing blood. "It's just a scrape. I tried to push the trunk open and must have caught my finger on something—"

"Let me see."

Gently grasping her wrist, he turned her hand over so he could see the cut. His jaw tightened as a tantalizing whiff of her perfume rose to his nostrils.

"The cut's not deep, but you need something on it." His gaze locked briefly with hers. "And you're looking a little shocky."

She was also cold. That could be due to shock, but the storm had dropped the autumn temperatures by a few degrees, so he turned the heaters on, directing the vents so the warm air hit her legs and fanned her face.

Once he was satisfied that she was warming up, Damon swung out of the truck. He knew that Hennessey never went anywhere without a comprehensive medical kit. He had already checked out the cab, so it was probably in the large gear box bolted to the tray of the truck.

Moments later, the kit in one hand, he climbed back into the cab. His door shut with a compressed thud, closing out the swirling cold air and moisture. Jenna's gaze locked with his, and suddenly the cab seemed too small and way too claustrophobic.

Dragging lean fingers through his soaked hair, he opened the first aid kit and extracted a hand towel, a box of bandages and a tube of antiseptic cream, but when he moved to pick up her right hand, she forestalled him. "I can do that."

Grabbing the hand towel, she pressed it onto her finger. Once the area was dry, she smeared antiseptic over the cut. She tore the packaging off the Band-Aid but, in her haste, the bandage slipped from her grasp and tumbled to the floor. Color flared along her cheekbones as she retrieved the now mud-smeared Band-Aid.

"Leave it," Damon said in a clipped voice. "You'll need a fresh one anyway."

Her gaze touched on his, and the edgy tension that gripped him morphed into burning heat.

"Damn," he muttered, "I wasn't going to do this."

It was his wedding day.

The last thing he needed to do was kiss his ex.

A wave of heat went through Jenna as Damon's hand cupped her nape and his head lowered. That was the point at which she should have scooted over in the seat, opened the truck door and stepped out into the weather. The only problem was the tingling heat from his palm at her nape and the way his gaze pinned her in place sent an all-too-familiar tension zinging through her.

Intellectually, she knew she should move, but her body refused to cooperate. Instead, she drew in a deep breath, which was a mistake, because her nostrils filled with the clean scent of his skin and the tantalizing hint of his cologne.

It was a heady mix, but then with Jenna, scent had always been a thing. It was an important indicator of whether she could be close with someone, and a lot of times it was the deal breaker with a date. She never told the guys who failed the olfactory test, but it was either very good, as in delicious, or it was *bad*, and before she could stop herself, she actually made a small noise and muttered, "Whoever sells that cologne must be making a fortune."

His head dipped and his mouth touched hers. As kisses went, it was light, almost fleeting, or it would have been if she hadn't wound an arm around his neck and melted into his arms. As the kiss deepened, a hot pang shot through her and any thought of resistance dissolved. Angling her jaw, she kissed him again.

A split second later, her phone chimed, she stiffened and he lifted his head. Fumbling for her phone, suddenly too mortified to even look at Damon—because she couldn't believe she had actually kissed him back—she answered the call.

Crazily, stuck in an isolated rural location, waiting for a hurricane to make landfall, it was a call from her PA in the office, wanting to confirm if she had agreed to do the Hollister wedding, which was scheduled in six months' time.

By the time she was off the call, Damon was driving, which was a relief, because she needed a minute. Averting her gaze from his clean profile and the five-o'clock shadow that darkened his jaw, she grabbed a handful of fresh tissues from her tote. Using the vanity mirror on the window shade, she wiped smudged mascara from beneath her eyes with hands that were just a little shaky.

The unsteadiness was patently not her. But the encounter with the ditch, then Damon, hadn't helped. And she just hadn't expected to react to him so strongly.

She touched her mouth, which was still tingling. She felt unnerved, almost flustered, because she had lost it so easily.

And there was her problem. The issue that had been keeping her awake at night, making her worry about Chloe and making her dread this wedding.

She still wanted Damon. Like, *really* wanted him.

And, unless she had gotten things totally wrong, she was pretty sure he still wanted her.

Six

Damon strode to his suite, peeled out of his soaked clothing and stepped under a cold shower for long minutes. When the unruly desire that had drawn every muscle in his body tight finally eased, he wrapped a towel around his waist, searched out dry clothing and quickly dressed.

He stared into the mirror that was suspended over his bedroom dresser as he knotted his tie. For the first time in a long time—*years*—the face that stared back at him reminded him of his father, Cole Wyatt.

And he knew why that was—he had kissed Jenna.

The feel of her mouth against his, the way her arm had curled around his neck, pulling him close for a second, deeper kiss as she'd melted against him made every muscle in his body tighten and spun him back to their last fling.

Two months of unrelenting temptation that he hadn't been able to resist, despite knowing that he needed to concentrate on the business of contracting a short-term paper marriage and interviewing possible convenient brides. Two months during which he had made constant excuses to be absent from Houston so he wouldn't get drawn deeper into the whirlpool of desire that Jenna inspired. The kind of obsessive, fatal attraction that had broken his father and which he had sworn off.

Ten years ago, according to Henry Beaumont, going after Jenna, who came from money and who would marry money, had made him like his father.

Damon hadn't wanted to agree. Beaumont had been a stiff-necked traditionalist and more than a little insulting. But the thought had stuck, because it was a fact that he and Jenna came from different worlds, the abyss between them wide enough, he hadn't ever believed that she would stay with him.

Admittedly, his inheritance had changed the equation: he didn't have the country club status, but he now had money.

However, their recent two-month fling hadn't changed his mind about the viability of a real relationship, even if he had wanted to take that risk. The passion aside, Jenna had been just a little too focused on his new wealth and the help he could potentially give her firm.

And she hadn't left it there. When he hadn't responded to her tentative suggestion that he could invest in Beaumont Law, she had hedged her bets by casting out lures to a string of wealthy lawyers, including Henderson, dating up a storm when he was out of town as she had tried to entice wealthy players into her family business.

Which was why kissing her now, when he was, finally, on the verge of marrying his convenient bride and fulfilling the terms of his uncle's will, was so wrong.

He was on the point of leaving the bedroom when he remembered that Jenna had said something about his cologne. Wearing it was something he did automatically these days, because his uncle had been something of a stickler for grooming and had insisted Damon get used to wearing a good cologne. He picked up the small, expensive bottle. Always before, he had seen it as an adjunct to getting dressed, but if Jenna liked it...

Jaw locking, he replaced the bottle on the dresser.

Minutes later, he strode out into his lounge, with its full frontal view of the brown and turgid Pleasant River, and it hit him anew that he could have lost Jenna.

And there was his problem, he thought grimly. Despite logic and common sense, despite years of staying away, he still wanted her, and seeing how close she'd come to disaster had made that fact hit home.

The accident itself hadn't been bad. She had simply lost control and ended up in the ditch. But if she'd had the same accident *on* the bridge, the SUV might have broken through the railings and gone into the water.

It hadn't happened, but the thought of Jenna, trapped in her SUV in the water was sharp and visceral, tightening every muscle in his body.

It was instantly followed by the clear and certain knowledge that despite his every effort to end what he could only term a fatal attraction, he had never succeeded. Not ten years ago, not six years ago and not now.

Despite the years that had passed, his desire for Jenna hadn't died, as it had with every other casual liaison. If anything, it had grown more intense, to the point that he'd had trouble maintaining his usual control when he had kissed Jenna.

And, like the attraction that had held his parents in thrall, he was aware that there was an addictive element. He couldn't resist her.

One thing was certain—his strategy of walking away had failed, spectacularly, on a number of occasions, for the simple reason that he had never stopped wanting Jenna.

He was also abruptly certain that he had hurt her.

She hadn't splashed the details of their relationship online because it hadn't mattered to her. And she hadn't inserted herself into his wedding then kissed him in his truck because she didn't care.

Despite the fact that he had walked away from her a month ago, despite his engagement to Chloe, Jenna still wanted him.

And, in that moment, his mind was made up. He had to get married today. That was a given: he would lose his inheritance if he stayed single. But he would figure things out with Jenna.

He would have to do some fast talking, and he would have to make it up to her, *if she would let him*. But, no matter what, he wasn't walking away, cold, this time.

His decision settled in. His feelings for Jenna had always been curiously black and white, and they weren't just sexual. It was a fact that he would rather cross swords with her than have a smooth, uncomplicated date with any other woman. It was a fact that she fascinated him.

They would have to wait until his marriage was dissolved before they could share a bed again, but their relationship had survived longer periods apart. One thing seemed clear, neither of them would be free until they let the attraction run its course.

Picking up his phone, he checked his calls.

Caleb had phoned him earlier, but he must have missed it while he was in the shower. He hit Caleb's number. Moments later, he picked up.

The upshot of the conversation made Damon's fingers tighten on the phone. Caleb had picked Chloe up. She was in Ransom, but she wasn't coming to the lodge, because she had changed her mind—she no longer wanted to get married.

Damon's stomach hollowed out. As the day had progressed, he'd developed a sinking feeling about Chloe, who, by her own admission, was spoiled, entitled and used to having and doing whatever she wanted.

Too late to realize he should have listened to his instincts. "The reason?"

"Uh—apparently, it's me." There was a small vibrating silence. "She thought marrying you would make me jealous."

Damon stared at the now heavy rain pounding the bank of bifold doors, turning the day dark. "So that was what all the wedding arrangements were about."

"Looks like," Caleb muttered. "By the way, I've just heard that the Pleasant River Bridge is flooded, so I'll stay the night in Ransom, wait out the storm and be in touch in the morning. And don't sweat it about the marriage deadline. Alan's will has a codicil around acts of God and natural disasters impeding the marriage. Since the storm is a category-two hurricane, that buys us another day or two."

A little grimly, Damon thanked Caleb and terminated the call. Dealing with Chloe had been, to say the least, frustrating. But if she no longer wanted to get married, there was nothing he could do about it.

After all, as Jenna had informed him, it wasn't the Dark Ages.

He was familiar with the codicil that Caleb had mentioned. That being the case, the hurricane had bought him a small window of time before he lost his inheritance.

And Chloe jilting him might not be a total disaster, because there was another option.

He could marry Jenna.

Six weeks ago, she had asked him if he was interested in investing in Beaumont Law which was on the brink of going under, because the last of the old partners had retired and every time Jenna recruited a new young lawyer to take the workload, within a few months they seemed to get better offers from other firms and disappeared.

After bleeding her own business dry to support the family law firm, Jenna was in desperate need of staff, a managing partner and an injection of cash. As strong and successful as she seemed, she was caught between a rock and a hard place.

And, suddenly, his mind was made up. He had already decided he wanted Jenna back in his bed, period, and damned if he would let Henderson cut in on him this time. Added to that, he needed a wife *today*, and Jenna was here and in need of help he was in a position to give.

He could solve Jenna's problems—if she would let him—by doing what he'd almost done a month ago: ask Jenna to marry him.

It was a gamble, but he had learned to trust his instincts. And right now they were telling him that, as unpromising as it would have seemed just hours ago, a marriage deal with his former lover could be done.

He found himself back at the bifolds, staring out at the storm, which was slowly but steadily building in intensity. The sensations that had burned through him when he had kissed Jenna replayed.

His fingers curled into fists. For ten years, he'd had difficulty maintaining any real interest in the women he had dated, because he had never forgotten what it had been like with Jenna.

Once the convenient marriage was over, Jenna Beaumont would be back in his bed for as long as it took for this inconvenient attraction to burn itself out.

He didn't know if she would agree to the marriage, or a relationship afterwards. He didn't know if he could resist her for a whole two months.

Marriage wasn't the ideal solution.

But from where he was standing, it was the only solution.

An hour later, and after a long hot soak in the bath, Jenna walked out of the bathroom wrapped in her cozy robe, a towel around her hair. She felt almost human again, although it couldn't wash away the guilt that she had actually *kissed* Damon.

Aside from betraying her own cousin, and doing something she personally abhorred—going after someone else's man—in terms of the wedding planner code, she had betrayed a client. She should be sent to Outer Mongolia to organize weddings for free, she should be boiled in oil—

Her phone pinged.

Dragging the cell out of her bag, she checked the screen. Chloe's name flashed. While she'd been in the bath there had been two missed calls from her cousin, and just now she had received a text message.

While she was holding the phone, it rang. Her stomach tightened. The guilt she was feeling for kissing Damon was actually making her feel sick, so Chloe was the last person she wanted to speak to, but she couldn't not answer the call.

Despite the horrible, guilty tension, she put a smile on her face, because apparently when you smiled, it made your voice sound happier, even if you were dying inside.

She picked up the call. "Chloe! Where *are* you? The wedding's in two hours."

The professional, wedding planner side of her desperately wanted the bride-to-be to get to the lodge quickly, and for the wedding to be over so she could get them safely married and put her mistake in kissing Damon behind her.

The only problem was, that wasn't all she was feeling.

The other part of her—the part that had practically flung herself at Damon and drowned in the kiss, then had gone back for seconds—didn't want Chloe to show, *ever*, which made her a very bad person.

"I'm in Ransom," Chloe said in a voice that sounded oddly calm and just a little cagey, as if she wasn't stressing about being late at all. "I flew in, apparently just before the airport closed, because some hurricane is going to hit. But we also found out that some weird little bridge out there is flooded, so... I can't make it to the wedding."

For a long moment, Jenna thought she had misheard. She had spent the last week centered on this wedding—a wedding she thought shouldn't be happening—and now it was off?

Trying to suppress a completely unprofessional surge of relief that actually made her knees feel as limp as noodles, she sat down on the edge of the bed. She picked up on something else Chloe had said. "We? Who's with you?"

There was a small hesitation. "Um… Caleb. He came looking for me at the airport and offered to drive me to the lodge—"

"I don't get it," Jenna said flatly. "Why did your *ex* go after you and not Damon?"

There was another small silence. "Well, maybe I *texted* Caleb…"

Suddenly, Jenna felt like she was forty and a parent dealing with a wayward teenager. With Chloe, that happened a lot. "Why would you text Caleb when you could have texted Damon? Or me? I was in Ransom a couple of hours ago. *I* could have given you a lift."

"Because I needed to speak to Caleb, just in case he thought I was making a horrible mistake."

Jenna frowned. She had the sense that her cousin was talking in some kind of weird code and she was missing the real meaning. "Of course you're very probably making a horrible mistake. We've had this conversation before. You barely know Damon so marrying him is a huge risk. And why would you want Caleb's opinion? I thought you two were finished?"

"We were. *Are*," Chloe muttered. "But I was hoping that, you know…with the wedding preparations and all, that he might…"

Jenna could feel her stomach sinking. Suddenly, it was all coming clear. "You wanted to make him jealous so he would want you back."

"That was the general idea, but it's backfired. We had a huge fight. Even though he does still want me, Caleb's crazy mad that I've ruined Damon's wedding plans and now he's walked out on me."

Jenna frowned. "So…you're still in love with Caleb?" With Chloe, one never knew. Emotions seemed to move like quicksilver through her life. If Jenna dated at the rate she did, she would be permanently dizzy.

There was a small hesitation. "The thing is, I'm pregnant. It's Caleb's baby."

For a split second, Jenna wondered again if she'd misheard, then relief that it wasn't Damon's baby flooded her. She found herself standing up when she couldn't remember doing so. Her mind was going a million miles an hour. She was still confused, because if Chloe was fixated on Caleb, she had no clue why she was marrying Damon. Or why Damon was marrying her.

Added to that, she didn't know whether to feel relief that her cousin hadn't slept with Damon and wasn't having his baby, or compassion that she was pregnant by a man who didn't love her. "Do your parents know?"

"Not yet. Aside from my doctor, nobody knows except you—"

"So that's why you couldn't be bothered with any of the details for the wedding—" One clear thought surfaced. "Does Caleb know you're pregnant?"

"*No*. I wanted him to love me before he found out about the baby."

"What about Damon?"

"Why would he know? I never intended to marry him. He only wants to marry because his dead uncle is forcing him to do it to get his inheritance."

Jenna blinked away an image of a zombie Alan Wyatt calling the shots from beyond the grave. But, suddenly it all made blinding sense. Damon's contention that he needed a wife, the lack of emotion around getting married and his annoyance at all the high-end wedding trimmings.

She felt as if a weight the size of a house had been lifted from her shoulders, because she wasn't a home-wrecker after all. And the fact that Chloe was not sleeping with Damon was crucially important because it meant the kiss today—and the intensity she'd glimpsed in Damon's eyes—had been *real*.

A flash of the heated intimacy of those moments in Hennessey's truck briefly welded her to the spot. Taking a deep breath, she forced herself to concentrate on Chloe. "So…you and Damon are not—?"

"No way! Why would I go after Damon when I'm in love with Caleb?"

Jenna found herself standing at the floor-to-ceiling glass doors in her sitting room, staring out at the driving rain. But the intensifying storm was nothing compared to her inner turmoil.

She had been feeling horribly guilty for betraying Chloe by kissing Damon, and for still wanting him. She had been prepared to feel even more awful, because it was beginning to look like Chloe could miss her own wedding. But the "bride" had spent the day trying to get Caleb—the father of her child—back, in which case, apparently, she had been prepared to leave Damon in the lurch.

Jenna was beginning to feel like she was living in a soap opera. "How on earth did you end up pregnant? I thought you were careful—"

"I *am* careful, normally. But when I'm with Caleb, he kind of pins me with those dark eyes and my brain switches off, and I stop thinking." There was a small, tense silence. "It's hard to explain," Chloe mumbled, "but if you ever fall in love, you'll know what I mean."

Jenna's fingers tightened on the phone. "How do you know I've never fallen in love?"

"Because the way you date is like… What's that numbers game you play?"

"Sudoku."

"That's it, numbers and boxes. You figure out guys and then you put them in boxes, and nothing *ever* adds up—"

"Sudoku adds up. That's the whole point."

"Not when I do it."

Jenna held the phone slightly away from her ear. Chloe was understandably upset, but listening to her was beginning to make Jenna crazy.

Taking a calming breath, she switched into the

soothing cadences she used with jittery brides. "Look, I'm really sorry that things haven't worked out with Caleb, and that you're stressed over the pregnancy. And I understand that you wanted to make Caleb jealous. What I don't understand is why you agreed to *marry* Damon."

"I never intended to marry him," Chloe said flatly. "Why would I when he should have asked you? I mean, you and Damon were together for, like, *two months*. And I know you still like him, like, *really* like him. But the thing is, he needs to get married, by midnight tonight—if he doesn't, he's going to lose all his money."

Jenna frowned. The crazily rushed wedding was, finally, beginning to make sense. She shook her head, hardly able to believe what Chloe was telling her, because the concept was so archaic. "A marriage of convenience?"

"To fulfill the terms of Alan's will. Apparently, he thought Damon should get married."

And suddenly the tension that had been building the closer she got to the wedding day—along with a bone deep misery she had done her level best to ignore, because it meant she hadn't managed to shake her feelings for Damon—dissolved, making her feel a little giddy.

Damon didn't want Chloe.

"There's just one more thing," Chloe said in an oddly tentative voice.

Jenna's stomach tensed again, because she suddenly knew *exactly* what her cousin was going to say.

"Since Damon still needs to get married and you're probably the only single woman—if not the only woman—at the lodge, I thought that *you* could marry him!"

Seven

Marry Damon because she was the only woman at the flooded-in lodge and he was out of options?

The thought shouldn't be so riveting, especially after the way he had discarded her then chosen Chloe as his bride!

Heart pounding, Jenna terminated the call, walked back into her bedroom and left the phone on her bedside table.

She couldn't believe it. Chloe, her sweet, often ditzy little cousin, whom Jenna had clearly made the mistake of confiding in when her last fling with Damon had crumbled, had set her up. And she had been so distracted by the way Damon had, apparently, swapped her out for her younger cousin, that she hadn't been able to read the clues.

Now, suddenly, the reason Chloe had used Jenna's list of her own personal wedding must-haves, including the cake and the dress, all of which had been posted on Beaumont's website, made perfect sense.

Like a chip off their great-grandmother's block, Chloe hadn't been either lazy or in a rush—she had been ruthlessly, methodically arranging *Jenna's* wedding.

But, if Damon had only needed a marriage of convenience, why hadn't he asked her in the first place?

The hurtful answer popped into her head almost immediately.

Because he had probably thought she would try to make the marriage real and, clearly, he didn't want that from her.

Feeling tense and unsettled, she found the fresh clothes she needed then walked back into the bathroom. After quickly dressing in a fresh pair of jeans, a cotton tank and a blue cashmere sweater, she set about drying her hair until it fell in soft waves around her shoulders.

With the wedding now off, she took her time applying light makeup. When she was done, she stared at her reflection. She looked almost exactly the same as she had that morning.

A small, sensual shiver swept her.

Except for the faint, telltale swelling of her mouth and a patch of redness on her chin where Damon's stubble must have scraped against her tender skin.

A marriage of convenience to Damon?

She drew a steadying breath. When she got married, *if* she ever got married, it would be to someone who cared for her enough that he would court her and spoil her and shower her with all the little gifts that women liked, including jewelry. All the special little things Damon had never done.

So, why couldn't she stop thinking about the crazy, tempting possibility that she could actually marry him?

Hanging her bathrobe on the hook at the back of the bathroom door, she walked back out to her bedroom, ending up at the window again. Her gaze was automatically drawn to the swollen river that had breached its banks and had already crept partway up the lawn.

Where men were concerned, she had always been spoiled for choice. The problem was she had been pampered from the cradle and she had been an only daughter, so, of course, she had been Daddy's girl. And with every guy she had dated—aside from Damon—she had gotten to pick and choose whom she wanted and for how long.

It was also, weirdly, one of the reasons she had found Damon so irresistibly attractive, because, whether he was in jeans and a Stetson or a business suit, there was no way he would be either picked up or discarded.

It was curious, then, that he was the only guy she had ever fallen head over heels for, and the only one she had ever gone back to.

The problem was that as a college varsity cheerleader, when she had walked out onto the Cougars practice field and seen Damon, hot and sweaty in his tight uniform, she had fallen for him. She had thought it was just a crush but, looking back, from that point on, everything had changed. The way she saw it now was that he had imprinted himself on her so strongly, she had never been able to fall for anyone else.

Just three weeks ago, she had found out from, of all people, Chloe—because, apparently Jenna's father had confided in hers—that the reason Damon had walked after the one night they had spent together back then was that her father had warned him off.

That one salient fact explained not just why Damon had finished with her so abruptly when she was nineteen, but why, six years ago, he had walked away from her again when she had tried to bring their second-chance relationship out into the open.

It occurred to her that if her father, who'd had a controlling streak a mile wide, hadn't intervened, their relationship might have progressed naturally. Instead, they had never gotten to date one another in the normal way, never gotten to argue and fight and sort issues out as most couples did, but had ended up stalled in the passionate honeymoon phase.

She had to wonder, if they'd been allowed to have a real, visible relationship, would they have tired of one another? Or, would the attraction have deepened, and they might have ended up married?

She drew a swift breath at that last thought, because their two months together, and the kiss in Damon's truck that morning, had highlighted that what she felt for him was definitely different than what she'd felt for any of her other dates.

And there was her problem. Damon was the reason she had utterly rejected the idea of marrying Brad six years ago. And she was suddenly certain that he was the reason she could not seem to fall for anyone else.

Just this morning, if he had asked her to marry him, her answer would have been a resounding no. But, between then and now, she had finally figured out why he had rejected her, and the answer was breathtakingly simple.

He had gotten the message that she was off-limits, maybe even that he wasn't good enough for her, and his black-and-white, alpha male response had been to walk away.

But years had passed. She had changed, and Damon, as the head of the Wyatt empire, had definitely changed. He was no longer Ransom's bad boy—he was older, more seasoned and muscular, a businessman with a habit of command that sat easily on his shoulders.

Before her rescue that morning, and that kiss, any thought that she and Damon had a future hadn't existed. But now she knew that, despite everything that had gone wrong, he did still want her.

It wasn't enough for a relationship; it certainly hadn't been in the past. But the idea that a marriage of convenience could give them the chance to build a real relationship was…tantalizing.

She didn't know if it would break down Damon's walls, the invisible barriers that seemed to stop them from ever progressing beyond passion, but, at the very least, it would get rid of the idea that she was off-limits.

It would be a huge risk to her heart, because it was a fact that where Damon was concerned, she had always been vulnerable.

Only one thing was certain, she thought grimly. If Damon did want to marry her—even if only to secure his inheritance—he was going to have to crawl across broken glass to make it happen.

Ten minutes later, after cleaning the mud off her leather boots and leaving them to dry in the bathroom, she decided she had better check that the wedding dress, which would now have to be returned, was undamaged. She had just lifted the lid on the gorgeous, horrendously expensive dress when her phone rang.

It was Damon, and he wanted a meeting with her down in the library.

Her heart thumped once, hard against the wall of her chest. She went hot, then cold, then hot again. After her call with Chloe, there could only be one topic of conversation.

Feeling on edge but curiously calm, Jenna strolled downstairs to reception. Of course there was no one there because, thanks to the weather, the lodge was practically deserted. Walking into the small office behind reception, she checked a floor plan that was pinned on the wall and marked where the library was.

Taking her time, she strolled down a corridor, found a set of mahogany doors with the legend *Library* inscribed on a brass plaque and walked in.

Her stomach tensed as she noted that Damon, looking fresh from the shower in a dark suit with a white linen shirt and blue tie, was seated at a desk going over some papers.

His gaze clashed with hers. "Thanks for coming down."

Minutes later, after directing her to a private elevator, he showed her into what must be his own suite, a masculine but airy space that looked like it had been taken straight from the pages of a glossy spa magazine. As Damon strode through the sleek, minimalist room, she suddenly saw him in a way that she hadn't before.

Not as the tough loner she had risked spending a summer with, or the enigmatic lover who had walked out on her a month ago, but as the seasoned, cosmopolitan businessman who ran Wyatt Industries.

The abrupt shift in perception was a jolt.

The changes that had taken place—and that she'd done her level best to ignore—were evident in the sleek, short haircut, the sexy cologne, the low-key but expensive clothing and the cool equanimity of his gaze. Added to that, she knew that he had graduated with a business degree and that for the past few years he had been gradually assuming control of Alan Wyatt's impressive business empire.

Just a couple of weeks ago, she had stumbled across a financial magazine that had profiled Damon's transition into Wyatt Industries, noting that, when Alan Wyatt had died, he had stepped into the role with ease, because he had been doing the job for the past five years. In addition, his own business interests had dovetailed with the fortune he had inherited, including an impressive share portfolio and a cutting-edge company that specialized in developing clean fuels and sustainable energy solutions.

He indicated she should sit on a linen couch. Too on edge to sit, she followed him into the roomy designer kitchen that was part of the flow of the big room and watched as he made coffee.

Once the grounds were filtering and the rich aroma filled the air, he leaned against the kitchen counter and crossed his arms over his chest. "I take it that by now Chloe's told you that she never intended to go through with the wedding."

Jenna kept her expression smooth. "She called about fifteen minutes ago."

"Then, I guess she must have also told you that the reason she doesn't want to marry me is that she wants Caleb back?"

And just like that, Jenna's efforts to be neutral and detached, to not reveal her see-sawing emotions that Damon was about to propose to her, *but only because he was being forced to do it,* evaporated. She sent him a fiery glance. "What I don't get is why you proposed marriage to Chloe in the first place, when you knew she and Caleb had had a relationship."

Damon's expression was remote. "Caleb said the relationship was over, and since it's only a legal arrangement for a period of two months, I didn't see a problem."

"Which is why, of course, you didn't want the flowers—"

"Or the cake, or the wedding arch. Or the bridal suite." He shrugged. "Chloe knew it was a basic, no-fuss wedding with a justice of the peace presiding." He retrieved a carton of milk from the fridge, poured coffee into mugs and handed her one, pushing the milk in her direction. "I suppose you thought I was trying to deprive her of a proper wedding."

Jenna's cheeks warmed as she poured milk. "In my family the rituals matter."

And the ritual of marriage mattered to *her*, because it signified love and care and a true giving of oneself to the other, the kind of commitment she longed for and which Damon seemed more than willing to bypass. Just as he bypassed the thoughtful gifts and touches that gave pleasure and warmth to a relationship.

Jenna wrapped her hands around the mug and took a sip. The aromatic coffee suffused her with instant warmth, making her realize that breakfast had been hours ago and that so much had happened, she hadn't thought to eat.

Damon took a mouthful of his coffee and set it down on the counter. "I have a proposition for you. I know you need someone to take on a senior partnership with Beaumont Law until Luke is ready to take over. If you'll agree to a marriage of convenience with me for a two-month period, I can guarantee you a partnership buy-in and a top-flight lawyer for a minimum period of three years." He shrugged. "I know it's an unusual request, but the fact is, I have a deadline—I have to meet the terms of Alan Wyatt's will by midnight tonight. If I don't, I could lose Wyatt Industries."

Even though she'd been prepared for it, the shock of the proposal—no, not proposal, she corrected herself, *proposition*—froze her in place. She realized, she had expected more—more warmth, more intimacy. "Let me get this clear," she said carefully. "Now that Chloe's let you down, you've decided you want to marry *me*?"

His gaze was wary. "It's a solution. For us both."

And in that moment she had a vivid flashback to the early hours of the morning after the last night they had spent together. She had thought he was going to ask her something momentous, maybe that he was even going to suggest she should move in with him. She realized she had been almost right. "You were going to ask me a month ago. Then you changed your mind."

His gaze locked with hers. "Because we were involved. This is a cut-and-dried business arrangement."

"But it's a fact that, whenever you and I get together, we usually do a whole lot more than share space." She met his gaze squarely. "What happens if we make love?"

Heat flared in his gaze. It was gone so quickly that, if they hadn't kissed earlier, she might have thought she had imagined it. But they *had* kissed, which meant that, however reluctant he was to admit it, Damon did still want her.

The thought made her pulse race and was a revelation that changed everything. Three times before, Damon had walked away from her clean, or so she had thought. But the kiss in his truck, on what was supposed to be his wedding day to another woman, said otherwise.

Despite the hurtful breakups, he not only still wanted her, *she was abruptly certain he had wanted her all along*, and she was in exactly the same boat.

The idea that this marriage would finally give them some time together in which to grow a real relationship took deeper root.

It occurred to her that in giving Damon sex so quickly every time they got together, she had made the basic error of bypassing the courting process. It was an error that she had never been even remotely tempted to make with anyone else.

To put it bluntly, Damon had gotten her without having to do much at all.

When she had originally fallen for him, she had seen him as an escape from the rituals and traditions of courting that had been so important to her family. But now, at twenty-eight, almost twenty-nine, she understood the value of those rituals, because they affirmed love and family and true intimacy, not just sex.

On that basis alone, it occurred to her that the two months' marriage provided them with the perfect opportunity to finally do just that—to get to know one another.

And, suddenly, her mind was made up.

Two months with Damon.

It would be a risk to her heart, but she was tired of never truly connecting with him, of feeling as if she was stuck in an emotional limbo. She was tired of being alone.

Thirty was looming and, despite being so focused on her business, she *wanted* marriage, home, hearth and babies, the whole kit and caboodle. She had been beginning to think she wouldn't have any of those things, and maybe she wouldn't have them with Damon, but she needed to try.

She would probably get hurt, but she had been hurt before. And, at least this time, she would *know*.

Lifting her chin, she met his gaze. "Yes."

Damon's gaze darkened, reminding her of the passion that seemed to explode between them at the drop of a hat. Taking a deep breath, she tamped down on emotions and sensations that, right now, she couldn't afford to feel. "Before I sign anything, I'll need to know what, exactly, the marriage entails."

In a deep, curt voice, Damon briefly outlined the main points.

Basically, it was a matter of sharing his River Oaks mansion in Houston for a couple of months. Other than that, she could continue her life as usual, just as he would.

"So all we do is *share* your mansion?"

"As a legally married couple." He hesitated, then mentioned a figure, which subtly shocked Jenna.

Her brows jerked together. "Did you offer Chloe money?"

"No."

"I didn't think so." With careful precision, she set her coffee down on the kitchen counter. "Let's make one thing clear. I'm not marrying you for money. I need help with Beaumont Law. That's *all* I want."

"Fair enough. But before we can finalize things, you need to sign a document my lawyers drew up. I'll ask Hennessey to come up and be a witness." Damon walked through to the sitting room, flipped open a briefcase that was on the coffee table and handed her a stapled set of pages entitled Marriage Contract.

Her name was already on it, which was just a little annoying, because it meant that Damon had been sure enough of her to edit the document before she'd even agreed to the marriage. "Before I sign, I'd like to read it through."

Damon checked his watch. "There isn't exactly a lot of time."

Jenna lifted her brows. She was the daughter of a lawyer. She had learned in the cradle that you never signed anything without reading it first. Besides, it wouldn't do Damon any harm to wait. "I'm a fast reader."

While he called Hennessey, she sat down on the couch, made herself comfortable and flipped through pages, speed reading. First up there was the split assets, with neither having any claim on the other's, which made sense. Neither was she surprised to see that there was a time clause—eight weeks max— and the fact that the contract doubled as a separation agreement.

What took her attention was the legalese near the end of the contract, which stipulated shared living quarters with separate rooms, separate beds and separate bathrooms, even down to separate schedules for meals. It was clear that there was a zero tolerance for intimacy, and that there was definitely no sex. An entire page, which contained robotically worded definitions, was dedicated to outlining just what the no-sex thing looked like, just in case anyone was in doubt.

Despite the heavy reading—despite the veto on sex, which she just plain ignored, because she figured lovemaking was going to happen regardless—it filled her with an odd kind of hope. The document highlighted Damon's intention to marry someone he didn't want in his life. But, reading between the lines, it also highlighted the reason he hadn't asked her, which was because he *did* want her.

She set the contract down. "What happens if any of these rules gets…broken?"

Damon turned from the position he had taken up by the bank of bifold doors, jacket stretched across broad shoulders, hands in pockets. His brooding gaze touched on hers, sending an electrical tingle shooting down her spine. "Which rules did you have in mind?"

All of them.

A knock at the door broke the moment. Seconds later, Hennessey strolled in, giving her a wary glance.

Smiling tightly, she asked for a pen and signed her name where a number of small yellow stickers indicated, then flipped pages to make sure she hadn't missed a sheet.

She handed the agreement to Damon. "It reads more like a business deal than a marriage, but then that's the whole point, isn't it?"

He checked the pages. "There's no other reason I'd be getting married," he said flatly.

Eight

Jenna searched through her suitcase for something to wear. *To her own wedding.*

Because she was only here for two nights, she had her casual jeans, sweaters and a coat. For the actual wedding she had her blue Chanel suit, which was gorgeous, but which was buttoned-down and definitely work clothing. She had also packed a white shirt and a cocktail dress.

Taking her cue from Damon, who looked *GQ* perfect in a dark suit with white shirt and tie, she opted for the cocktail dress, which was a deep red jersey silk with bare arms and a cowl neck. Sleek and fitting, it always looked good. It wasn't exactly bridal, but then, this wasn't that kind of wedding.

But now that she had decided to use the marriage as a final attempt to spark a real relationship with Damon, despite his draconian marriage rules, what she wore *mattered*. Out of nowhere, the acute tension that had gripped her when they had kissed flared to life, making her pulse race and her stomach feel tight.

Drawing in a deep breath, she tried to control the emotions that were suddenly coursing through her, but now that they were out, she felt tinglingly alive, like a sleeper waking up. After years of disappointment that the only man she had truly wanted had never seemed to want to commit to her, she was on the verge of marrying him, and suddenly she was feeling too much—*wanting* too much.

Taking another deep breath, she shook out the cocktail dress and laid it across the bed. But before she slipped it on, she picked up Chloe's Vera Wang dress, which she had hung in the bathroom to get creases out, and laid that across the bed, too. It wasn't a big princess gown, but was a simple white silk shell with a strapless bodice and a silk tulle overlay that clung to the body and flared out from midthigh. It was gorgeously simple, crazy expensive and her current favorite wedding dress, which had made it all the more difficult when she'd known that Chloe was going to be wearing it when she married Damon.

And it was in her size.

Suddenly, feeling both emotional and suspicious, she checked the box the dress had come in, which also held a veil, a shoebox and a jewelry case. The gorgeous shoes were also her size, not Chloe's. When she opened the jewelry case, which held a delicate diamond and pearl necklace and a matching pair of earrings, a note popped out. *A gift for your wedding day. Love, Chloe.*

A lump formed in her throat. Feeling a little teary, because the dress was absolutely the right size, after all, she stepped into the dress and zipped up the back.

The cool silk of the lining settled against her skin, making her shiver. It fit perfectly. She slipped into the shoes, inserted earrings into her lobes and fastened the necklace.

Carrying the veil to the mirror, she fastened it with the jeweled clip provided and stared at the picture she made. The pure white silk and the floaty tulle veil gave her tanned skin a glow and made her eyes seem an almost incandescent shade of blue, but that wasn't what held her attention. With the shadowy hint of cleavage at the bodice and the silk tulle molding her waist and hips, she also looked startlingly sensual.

She stared at her reflection—the transformation from wedding planner to bride, electrifying.

For years now she had watched bride after bride get married, yet she hadn't considered what it meant to be the bride, how potent the moment could be.

Common sense said she should change out of the wedding gown and wear the cocktail dress instead, but the instant she considered doing just that, her jaw firmed. She hadn't planned for it, but this was *her* wedding. Given the way her relationships had gone lately, it might be the only wedding she ever had.

And given the way that Damon continually side-lined her, as if he didn't see her as someone to cherish and hold "until death do us part", maybe it was time he did see her this way.

A final check in the mirror and it hit her anew that in approximately thirty minutes, she would be married to Damon.

And, given the sexual chemistry that had sizzled between them that morning, the odds were slim to nonexistent that sex wouldn't be a part of this marriage.

The tension that had been building ever since she had agreed to the marriage lifted another notch.

With fingers that shook a little, she quickly redid her makeup, keeping it to a minimum but making her eyes just a little smoky, since it was evening. After winding her hair into a loose, messy knot, she refastened the veil.

Jenna briefly considered that the veil was too much, then discarded the thought. She had already decided to make a statement with the dress, so there was no point not wearing the veil. Or failing to collect the gorgeous bouquet that was stored downstairs in a cooler just off the kitchen.

After finding her small evening clutch, she dropped her room key in it and made her way downstairs. After retrieving the bouquet, she took a deep breath. She was under no illusions about what Damon would think when he saw her.

Keeping her expression smooth and her stride even, she stepped into the reception room where the ceremony would be held. Even so, she almost faltered when Damon's gaze clashed with hers.

He reached her in two strides, blocking out the rest of the room. "What do you think you're doing?"

Her chin came up. "Since this is my wedding," she said briskly, "exactly what I want." She lifted a brow at Damon's dark suit, dazzling white shirt and blue tie. "You're not exactly dressed for a quiet night in."

Dark amusement surfaced in his gaze. "This is not, exactly, a conventional marriage—"

"I know exactly what it is." Now thoroughly annoyed, she stepped close enough that she could feel the heat emanating off his big body, and brazenly wound her fingers around his tie and tugged lightly. "I've read the contract, all twenty pages of it. I know what it says we can and can't do."

Gaze narrowing, his hand closed over her fingers, sending a small electrical thrill clear through her. "Damn, what are you up to?"

A small cough broke the moment, and her stomach sank when she recognized Alan Wyatt's lawyer, Ron Parmentier. Ron was a retired partner of Beaumont Law who used to play golf with her father and who had practically rocked her cradle.

The other gentleman with him was also, unfortunately, very familiar. Hiram Chase was a county clerk, a justice of the peace and possibly the town's most effective gossip. His wife, Betty, a veteran of the Ransom County Women's Club, came in a close second. Between them, Hiram and Betty were the equivalent of the FBI, Mossad *and* the KGB. If there was anything that went on in Ransom, and Hiram and Betty didn't know about it, then it wasn't worth knowing. Six years ago, they had been mission control for the Jenna/Damon scandal.

Damon, who had released his grip on her fingers, sent her a glance, brimming with an irony that only the two of them would understand. If Hiram and Betty had besmirched her reputation, they had burned Damon's to a crisp.

His gaze dropped slightly, and her stomach clenched as another jolt of awareness hummed through her. If she had thought he would miss the modest cleavage on display, she would be wrong.

She smiled brightly at Ron and Hiram. Time for some damage control.

Had she wanted to keep this secret? For the short term, absolutely, because, after the incendiary material she had given Chantal Sanderson, news of the marriage, *just one month later*, needed to be carefully orchestrated. Her preference was to announce it through her own blog. However, if Hiram and Betty were online, all bets were off.

She shook Ron's hand first. Smoothly ignoring his curious gaze, she asked how his wife, Letitia, was doing. Keeping her expression serene, she turned to Hiram, who was clearly bursting with questions.

But before the man could probe for more gossip than the juicy tidbit he already had—that, just hours before the wedding, the bride had been switched out for a close relation, *shades of sister wives*—Damon's arm slipped around her waist.

The warmth of his touch and the casual possessiveness of the way he pulled her against his side, as if they were still lovers, sent another wave of desire through her.

"Since everyone's here," Damon said in a low, clipped voice, "we should start."

To her surprise he steered her in the direction of the wedding arch. A touch she had deliberately installed because she had been so annoyed that he was dating other women *and* marrying Chloe in a hunting lodge.

As the words of the marriage service were uttered, the wind continued to hit the lodge in waves, actually flexing the windows slightly, the changes in pressure making the candles flicker. As Jenna repeated vows and listened to Damon's, despite herself she became caught up in the depth and timeless beauty of the ceremony. When Damon took her hands in his, apart from the electrical tingle she felt at the contact, a wave of warmth and pleasure washed though her, making her go a little misty.

Hiram finished with a flourish, pronouncing them man and wife.

Jenna stared at him for a long moment. "We're not done." And if they were, it was the shortest wedding ever. "Where are the rings?"

Hiram froze like a deer caught in the headlights. "Uh—there are no rings."

Jenna wondered if she had stepped into the twilight zone. She had personally attended close to five hundred weddings in six years. Every time there had been rings. But, apparently, not for *this* wedding, and suddenly, all the pleasure she'd taken in a ceremony that was ancient, time-honored and sacred, and which had actually made her a little teary-eyed, evaporated. "The exchange of rings is an important part of the ceremony. To exclude them is…" She searched for the word and found it. "It's barbaric."

And, not to put too fine a point upon it but, like every other aspect of Damon's vision for this wedding, it was cheap.

Jenna removed her hands from Damon's. "Please tell me you have the rings in your pocket."

Rings went with the vows. They were a universally recognized sign. How would anyone know they were married without the rings?

And then the whole point of *no rings* hit.

As far as Damon was concerned, the fewer people who knew they were married, the better, because it would make it easier to dispense with the marriage— *and her*—in two months' time.

Despite her every effort to bolster herself against disappointment with this marriage, her positivity had just taken a huge hit. She had signed Damon's quite frankly insulting, rule-bound contract. And had gone into this wedding with a measure of hope, but it was fast sinking in that she hadn't married Jekyll.

She had married Hyde.

Damon's gaze was frustratingly unreadable. "You have to know that rings were never going to be a part of this ceremony."

Jenna stared at him for a long moment. If this

was a movie, right about now a sinister bell of doom would toll. "No wonder Chloe didn't get an engagement ring."

Minutes later, they had both signed the marriage decree. Hiram packed the papers away, and one of the waitstaff appeared with champagne and a tray of the smoked salmon canapés that Jenna's favorite chef had prepared.

She accepted a glass of champagne. Normally, she didn't do more than take an occasional sip, but, after the debacle of the rings, she felt she needed something, so she took a healthy swig.

Half a glass later, and with the party, such as it was, already breaking up, her phone chimed.

"Excuse me," she said, smiling tightly at Damon and Hennessey, who were deep in conversation about whether or not his dusty hunting trophies, which she had stacked in a convenient shed, would survive the storm.

Walking out to the front foyer, then on into a small private lounge, she picked up the call before it went to voice mail. It was Brad, which was a little disconcerting.

Lowering her voice, she asked him what he wanted and was mildly annoyed to discover that, instead of being tied up in LA, Brad was now in Houston and expected her to meet him for a drink.

"A drink at your apartment?" Everyone knew that was code for cheap, meaningless sex. "I don't think so," she said firmly. "In any case, I'm…working."

A split second later, the phone was taken from her hand.

"Henderson?" Damon said in a curt voice. "It's Damon Wyatt. Don't call her again, or try to get her to come to your apartment, because it won't be Jenna turning up, it'll be me."

He pressed the disconnect button and returned the phone, his gaze steely and remote enough to send a chill down her spine. "You didn't tell me you were dating that creep."

Jenna slipped the cell back in her clutch and tried to control the oddly primitive thrill that curled through her that Damon had not only come after her, but that he had gotten rid of Brad, backing up his flatly delivered command with the threat of a personal visit if need be.

But, as exhilarating as that was, it was the way he had let Brad know that she was his that had riveted her. His words had been blunt, declarative and definitively alpha.

After ten years of transient flings, Damon had finally done the one thing she had wanted him to do all along—he had *claimed* her.

"I'm not dating Brad," she said, meeting his gaze squarely. "He showed some interest in buying a partnership in Beaumont Law. Until the agreement I made with you, I had been considering it."

"Forget about Henderson. There's no need for him to be involved, period."

Her chin came up. She knew she should leave it, because she now didn't need or want Brad's help, but she wasn't inclined to let Damon treat her as if she didn't have a brain, and she was still upset about the rings. "Last I heard, marriage doesn't mean my IQ dropped or that I'm incapable of making decisions. If I want Brad involved, he will be involved."

His hand landed on the wall behind her head. "That'll be over my dead body," he said softly.

"Why?" she challenged, a sharp thrill shooting up her spine, because she already knew.

"This is why." And his mouth came down on hers.

The passion, already ignited in his truck, was white-hot and instant. Out of nowhere her heart began to pound, and not just because Damon's kiss was making desire shiver and burn through her, starting an all-too-familiar hot ache.

He was jealous. He'd been jealous of Brad six years ago, and he was jealous now.

That was a clear indicator that she *did* mean something to him and that maybe, just maybe, he was just as fixated as she. As she looped her arms around his neck and kissed him back, it occurred to her that six years ago, Damon's response to Brad had been to cut her loose—the exact opposite of what he was doing now.

As Jenna moved in closer still and went up on her toes, fitting herself against the hard planes of his body, the first kiss was followed by a second, then a third.

Damon's arm shot out and pushed the door of the small reception room closed, then they were moving by slow increments. The backs of her legs came into contact with the cool linen of a couch. He lifted his head, taking a moment to shrug out of his jacket.

Her veil floated to the floor and she felt his fingers in her hair, loosening pins. Another melting kiss and she felt the zipper of the gorgeous wedding dress give way. Moments later, she stepped out of the puddle of white silk in just her bra and panties.

Cool air making her shiver, she pulled his mouth back to hers, angling her jaw to deepen the kiss. Fingers moving feverishly, she dragged at his tie, opened the buttons of his shirt, then slid her palms lower over washboard abs to find the fastening of his pants. A tense moment later, she dragged down the zipper.

Damon muttered something flat beneath his breath. Seconds later, his hands cupped her breasts through the silk of her bra, and heat seared straight to her loins. Dimly, she felt her bra loosen, the soft drag as it was pulled from her arms. Cool air washed over her skin as he bent and took one breast into his mouth, and her fingers sank into the solid muscle of his shoulders as, for long moments, tension coiled and gathered…

"Not yet," Damon muttered grimly.

The world went sideways as he lifted her into his arms and laid her down on the couch. The shock of the cool linen against her skin made her abruptly aware of how far they had come, and how fast, but she was drowning in sensation and stopping wasn't an option.

Dimly, she noted that making love with Damon

was a huge risk—nothing could make her more vulnerable. And it was a crazy, total breaking of the marriage rules, because of all the rules they could break, this one would make the union real. It was the one thing Damon didn't want. But, after the pain of thinking she had lost him to, first, another anonymous woman, and then to Chloe, it was a risk she was prepared to take.

His gaze locked with hers and her heart squeezed tight. And there was her problem, she thought with sudden clarity. For ten years she had been stuck in limbo, unable to move on from Damon. The problem was he had been her first *and only* lover and every time she looked at another man, she unconsciously compared him to Damon.

He shrugged out of the shirt. In the dim lamp-lit room, he seemed broader and more muscular than she remembered, while at the same time his short, tailored haircut, the hint of a five-o'clock shadow on his jaw, added a sophistication that hadn't been there six years ago. It was a potent combination that literally sent a shiver down her spine.

His weight came down beside her. Another long, drugging kiss later and she felt the wash of cold air as her panties were peeled down her legs.

She had a brief moment to note the swiftness with which they had arrived at this moment, then Damon's mouth came down on hers again. Winding her arms around his neck, she fit herself more closely against him, and in that instant the last, hurtful month, and the six empty years that had passed before that, dissolved. Memories cascaded. Some vivid and heated, some with an unexpected sweetness.

Feeling oddly emotional and elated, because she loved making love with Damon, and she had missed this, missed *him*, she slid her fingers beneath the waistband of his pants and found him.

He groaned and said something flat beneath his breath. Unable to resist, Jenna shimmied closer on the awkward space of the couch, one arm around his neck, and both legs loosely twined around his hips, and felt him lodge at her entrance. A split second later, she tensed as, with a convulsive movement he slid deep.

She froze. Shock at the abrupt entry and an aching heat shimmered through her, molten and irresistible, taking her breath.

Damon uttered another muffled groan. His hands grasped her hips, holding her still, but it was already too late as she felt her body tightening around him.

She had a moment to log that things had moved so frantically fast that Damon was still half-dressed and there was no contraception, which was not like her, and definitely not like Damon. Whenever they had made love in the past, he had been scrupulously careful about sheathing himself, to the point that she had gotten the distinct impression that no way did he ever want to risk impregnating her.

His head came up; his gaze connected with hers. Something like shock flared in his gaze, and she felt the moment of coolness as he began to withdraw.

Damon was going to do the responsible thing,

sheath himself, something for which she should be thankful but, as she felt him withdraw, something in her rebelled. During the two months they had slept together, she'd been acutely aware that Damon never lost control but always held himself just a little distant and aloof. But that wasn't what she wanted from him now. Hurt by the way he had walked out on her just when she had thought they were finally becoming a couple, dazed by the intensity of the emotions that flooded her, she simply wanted Damon.

Closing her arms around his neck, she deliberately lifted against him, relief filling her as he pushed deep within her again. The risk of pregnancy flashed through her mind, but the thought dissolved as they began to move and pleasure, heated and irresistible, gripped her. The feel of Damon naked inside her, the raw intensity and the intimacy of what they were doing, closed out the cool dampness of the air, the howling wind outside and the heavy rain battering the windows.

Damon's head dipped, she felt the scrape of his teeth over one lobe and the heated tension low in her belly coiled and tightened before shuddering through her with an intensity that made tears burn at the back of her throat.

Long moments later, Damon, holding Jenna loosely against him, propped himself up on one elbow.

His gaze brooding and reflective, he studied the dark crescents of her lashes, ridiculously long against the pale curve of her cheeks, the glitter of diamonds at her lobes and the silken tangle of her hair. He couldn't believe he had lost control to the extent that they had made love without protection. It was the first time it had happened to him, and it had to be the last, he thought grimly.

Just minutes into the marriage and they had already broken the marriage agreement.

If Jenna was pregnant...

He stroked a finger down her cheek. Her lids flipped open. "How likely is it that you'll get pregnant?"

He felt her tense against him. "Not that likely, since I've probably ovulated already. I should have a period in a few days."

He drew a deep breath. "If you're pregnant—"

"If I'm pregnant, the marriage agreement covers the eventuality, so you don't need to worry about it." She met his gaze squarely. "It was my fault. I should have let you put on a condom."

Jaw tight, he had to restrain himself from reaching for her again as she disengaged from his hold, pushed up from the couch and quickly began dressing. Rolling to his feet, he fastened his pants, pulled on his shirt and jacket and folded the tie before shoving it in his pocket.

When they'd made love the very first time, Jenna had been a virgin, and that fact had rattled him. Now he was shaken anew because, the last thing he wanted to do was bring a child into a relationship that could only be temporary.

As Jenna shimmied into the white wedding dress

and zipped it up with an elegant, quintessentially feminine movement, she pinned him with a look he was beginning to recognize. She might have been born with a silver spoon in her mouth, but she was strong and independent, as self-sufficient as a cat. After first her father then her mother had died, she had made her own way, established her own business and supported her brother, which was no mean feat.

"I understand how this works," she said flatly. "If there is a baby, I'm perfectly capable of taking care of it. You don't have to be involved."

And, suddenly, the idea of 'temporary' when it came to Jenna, dissolved. "What if I want to be involved?" he growled.

Cupping her chin, he bent and kissed her briefly on the mouth. "Whatever happens, we'll work it out. But we can't have unprotected sex again."

The marriage contract was black-and-white about sex and pregnancy: the marriage would come to an end in two months' time, regardless of whether it was an annulment or a divorce. But, if Jenna were pregnant…

His fingers curled into fists. That changed things. He would not turn his back on his child.

He knew firsthand what *that* felt like.

An hour later, after seeing Jenna to her room, and still unable to sleep, Damon gave up on his tangled bed, pulled on jeans and a sweater, and strolled out to the kitchen.

He still couldn't believe that he'd lost control with

Jenna to the extent that they'd ended up making love without protection. But, the fact that Henderson had called Jenna with the intention of getting her into bed had literally made him see red.

Six years ago he had been on the verge of going toe to toe with Henderson on the street in Ransom, because he had been certain the older man was making a move on her. The very fact that he had almost started a fight in public had been startling in itself, because after years of dragging his father out of brawls, it was the one thing he had sworn off.

He filled a glass with water and drank it down in several long gulps, although the coolness of the water did nothing to alleviate the tension that gripped him. And in that moment, he noted how far he'd come with Jenna.

He wanted her back in his bed, but now that she was, he was beginning to want more. He could feel the possessiveness in him, the desire to place a corral around Jenna, to protect her.

It was a step into dangerous territory, because suddenly he was feeling too much and wanting too much because, despite the fiery attraction that bound the together, they still came from different worlds.

Henderson's phone call, *on his wedding day,* was a reminder of the dynamic that had played out between his parents, and that was now presently playing out between him and Jenna. And the bedrock fact that, once the passion faded, he couldn't trust that she would stay.

As he placed the glass in the dishwasher, a heavier

than usual gust of wind hit the side of the lodge, hard enough that the timbers creaked and something tore off with a shrieking whine.

Picking up his phone, he checked his weather app. The report wasn't good. The hurricane, which had started out in the Gulf of Mexico, had lost a little of its strength over the land, but not enough. They were still at a category two.

As he walked toward the glass doors of his sitting room, a second huge gust hit the lodge. More worrying, the continuing sound of shrieking metal signaled that the iron roof had sustained some damage. A split second later, a loud bang punctuated the whine of the wind as a tree branch hit the glass doors of his suite, sending a crack snaking from top to bottom.

At a guess, the branch came from the ancient oak that was the only tree close to the lodge. At that point, Damon knew what needed to happen next. He'd been through enough big storms to understand when one was dangerous.

He phoned Hennessey, who, like him, was still up. Then he walked to Jenna's suite and knocked on her door. She must have been awake, because she answered the door almost immediately in a silky, tightly belted robe, her sleepy eyes and disheveled blond hair somehow making her look even more gorgeous. Jaw tight, he tried to tamp down on his automatic response.

Her gaze latched on to his. "What was that loud bang?"

"A branch hitting the glass doors of my suite. You

need to get dressed and pack what you need for the night. The oak tree is a hazard, and I'm pretty sure the roofing iron is tearing at the south end of the lodge. Maybe that's as bad as it'll get, but just in case, we need to move into the cabins to make sure no one gets hurt."

"There are only three cabins—"

"And eight people, including kitchen staff, to go in them. Which is why you and I will be sharing one."

A little grimly, Damon noted that they'd already broken the marriage rules once. Looked like they were going to break them again.

Jenna crossed her arms over her chest, her gaze suddenly wide awake and challenging. "Are you sure you want to do that? Our track record with following your marriage rules hasn't exactly been good, since we've already broken clauses 10a and 10e."

"We won't be breaking 10e again," Damon said flatly. That was the unprotected sex and pregnancy clause. As for the no-sex clause… "But, damned if I'll be sleeping with Hiram and Ron. We'll just have to take our chances with 10a."

Nine

Jenna packed while Damon alerted the others in the building.

After stripping out of her silky night gear, she slipped into a cute set of pink lingerie that she couldn't help thinking was designed to break a whole lot of rules. Maybe it wasn't a helpful thing to do, considering the circumstances, but she just had not been notified to bring plain cotton underwear.

The way she saw it, she was just being herself, and why should she have to change just because she had somehow ended up married to Damon? And she was definitely not about to apologize for the fact that she liked to wear pretty underwear. Just because they were stranded together in a storm didn't mean she had to look bad.

She quickly changed into her jeans and a sweater, pulled on socks then laced up her still-damp leather boots. Grabbing her tote, she made sure to drop in her moisturizer and some makeup.

On impulse, she collected her perfume, which she knew turned Damon on, and spritzed herself with it before tossing that in the tote, too.

Maybe she was behaving badly by coating herself with irresistible pheromones, but the fact that he reacted to her perfume was just not her problem, and she didn't see why she should deprive herself of the gorgeous scent just because Damon had an issue.

Walking through to the bathroom, she rescued her coat, which was now mostly dry, and shrugged that on. Just before she exited her suite, she remembered the praline chocolates and dropped them into her tote. If she was going to be stuck in a rustic log cabin with Damon and trying to stick to a bunch of rules, she was going to need chocolate.

Damon, dressed in wet-weather gear and carrying a rucksack, met her at the foot of the stairs. As she fell into step with him, his gaze connected with hers in a possessive way that made her pulse race.

All the lodge occupants were gathered in the room in which the wedding had been held. Hennessey did a roll call, but it was Damon who took command. A part of the lodge roof at the southern end *had* been damaged, and the oak tree seemed to be losing branches. Everyone was allocated a cabin. Since they were also flooded in, hopefully by morning the weather should have cleared enough to get a helicopter in to take them all out.

Minutes later, they took a side entrance with a pathway that led to the cabins. As she stepped outside, the pressure of the wind pushed Jenna sideways. Damon, who had gone first, slung his arm around her waist, anchoring her against his side.

Using a heavy-duty flashlight, he illuminated the path ahead, which was strewn with debris. Light washed over a familiar cabin. With a sense of inevitability, she noted that it was the one she had prepared earlier.

Damon produced a key, unlocked the door and held it for her while she scooted inside. Seconds later, he slammed the door against the wind and rain, and they were enveloped in warmth and stillness.

"Don't tell me," he muttered. "The wedding suite."

Jenna peeled out of her wet raincoat. "Just remember, I didn't book it. Chloe did."

He dropped his rucksack on the floor and shrugged out of his oilskin. "At least we now know why."

"Which is a relief," she said, taking his oilskin and her coat through to the bathroom, "because her marriage to you just didn't make any kind of sense. Especially not with your dating schedule."

He came to lean against the door frame and watched as she draped their coats over the bath so they could dry. "You checked up on me."

"What did you expect? You ditched me for some other woman."

And she had been fairly ruthless about checking on Damon. She had tracked him like a bloodhound across Tinder and a number of other dating sites, *and* she had logged in to some exclusive chat rooms she had access to through her wedding planning business to see who, exactly, was talking about him.

Overall, it had been a depressing business, because Damon had literally dated more women than she'd had hot dinners.

His gaze narrowed. "That woman was my first convenient bride. The one who pulled out of the deal when certain details of our time together were leaked to some gossip columnist—"

"Don't expect an apology," she said shortly. "What you did *hurt*. That last night, I thought we were on the verge of finally having a real relationship, but when it came to marriage and commitment, *you chose someone else*."

Damon stepped into the bathroom, which had seemed large when she'd laid out the robes and the candle, but which now seemed to shrink, because, with his height and broad shoulders, Damon took up all the room.

"Because of this," His hands closed over her hips as he coaxed her close. "Babe, I knew I couldn't keep my hands off you."

Heat shimmered through Jenna, but she wasn't about to be fobbed off with more meaningless sex even if he had called her "babe."

Stepping easily out of his hold, she marched back out to the bedroom. "Back to the dating issue. I also know that you dated some redhead the day *after* you got engaged to Chloe."

She picked up her tote and retrieved her makeup bag and perfume. When she turned, intending to store the items on the dresser, she almost ran into Damon

"If you're talking about Amber Stevens, that wasn't a date—"

"Amber wasn't exactly dressed for a business meeting."

A mixture of frustration and amusement registered in his gaze. "You have to know it was a conference dinner."

She pretended she hadn't seen that glint of humor, because then she would have to get mad, and plowed on. "So, okay, Amber in her low-cut red dress was a *business acquaintance*. But, during the next week, while Chloe was on vacation, you dated Tiffany Styles, someone called Monica *and* Buffy Hamilton—"

Drawing a deep breath, she tamped down on the frustration and the wild vulnerability that had been building ever since they'd made love, but she guessed if she wanted Damon to make some kind of relationship progress, she had to let him see that the jealousy and possessiveness thing went both ways. He had been short with Brad, who, let's face it, she wouldn't touch with a ten-foot pole. But it also went without saying that if another woman tried to hit on Damon while they were married, she would not be found sitting at home watching TV.

He frowned. "Except for Monica, who's an old friend, those weren't dates. They were charity galas and oil conference dinners—" His gaze locked with hers. "What is it, exactly, that you want?"

"There was a clause in the marriage contract about dating, but it only applied to me. Don't think I didn't notice that there was no veto on your dating other women."

His brows jerked together. "I won't be dating anyone else while we're married. Why would I?"

She suppressed the sudden giddy delight that Damon was willing to nix his dating life for her, because she knew there was a codicil. "Only for the duration of the marriage?"

"Maybe longer," he muttered. "Damn, what is that perfume you're wearing?" And pulling her close, he finally did what she'd been dying for him to do— he kissed her.

When she finally came up for air, she stretched against him, her arms loosely coiled around his neck. "You're breaking the rules again."

"Since we already broke them once tonight," he murmured, dipping down to drag the edge of his teeth against one earlobe, "one more time won't make any difference."

This time when they made love, Damon was determined to go slow *and* use a condom.

His arms closed around her as he walked her in the direction of the bed. Aside from taking his time, they were also going to be comfortable.

Another drugging kiss, as Jenna went up on her toes and fitted herself against him, ratcheted up the tension another notch. He freed his mouth to strip off his sweater, then groaned as she slid her palms across his chest. Seconds later, he peeled Jenna's sweater over her head and stopped when he saw the lacy pink push-up bra. At a guess, it was designed to drive men crazy. In which case, he was now, officially, crazy.

Unlatching the bra, he bent down to take one breast into his mouth. Jenna pulled his head back to hers for another kiss and, long seconds later, stepped away to strip out of her jeans and a pair of pink panties that matched the bra.

A jolt went through him as she stepped close and unfastened his pants with a deliberation that made him tense and groan. When her hand slid down to grasp him for long seconds, he thought he wasn't going to make it to the bed.

Stilling her hand, he finished undressing, then found the condom. A split second later, Jenna wrapped her arms around his neck and kissed him, and then they were sprawling on the bed. But, his plans to take things slow crashed and burned when she straddled him, took the condom from his fingers and tore the foil. "This time," she said, meeting his gaze boldly, "it's my turn to be on top."

Ten

Gray morning light filtering through the linen curtains that shrouded the bifold doors of the cabin awoke Jenna from a deep, dreamless sleep. Stretching, she was instantly aware of the faint stiffness and small aches that went with unaccustomed lovemaking.

Rolling over, even though she sensed that Damon was no longer there, she was disappointed to encounter cool sheets and a note written on the lodge's letterhead. He had gone to check out the damage to the lodge and would be back shortly. A helicopter was due to fly in and pick them up at 9:00 a.m.

It was already eight, so she climbed from the bed, shrugged into her silk robe, quickly found a change of clothes and stepped into the en suite bathroom.

Her stomach tightened as the steamy warmth of the room and the condensation on the vanity mirror. Damon had obviously showered earlier, a fact that suddenly seemed unbearably intimate and drove home the knowledge that they were *married*. There would be no hurried goodbyes or hastily organized trysts, at least not for the next two months.

One hand strayed to her flat belly. Two months, during which she would discover whether she was pregnant or not.

Suddenly, the thought that she could be carrying Damon's baby sank in, making her feel breathless and just a little light-headed. Less than twenty-four hours ago she hadn't considered marriage, let alone a pregnancy. In the years she had been building up her business and trying to save Beaumont Law for Luke, she had been almost too busy to breathe. As much as she had wanted them for herself, marriage and babies had always been for others.

Now, the possibility that Damon's child might be growing inside her changed…everything. Apart from the fact that she was falling for him, *again*, the stakes might possibly be even higher, because if she was pregnant, it wasn't just all about her—she would have their baby to consider.

She had wanted a real relationship with Damon before. But, now, if she really was pregnant, then she absolutely had to get that relationship right.

A baby.

She wouldn't know anything for a while, but she needed to start planning for the possibility.

It occurred to her that, if she was pregnant, Damon could insist that they stay married. She knew something of his embattled past—the scars and the loss—and that, rather than being broken by the experience, he had emerged in strength as a protector. He would want to care for her and be part of his child's life. And, after the last twenty-four hours, she did want to stay married to Damon, *but not just because she was carrying his child.*

What she wanted was for Damon to not just want her sexually, but to need her in his life, to fall for her and love her for herself.

She had two months, during which they would be stuck together and he couldn't leave, in which to help him do just that.

And this time she had a plan.

Firstly, she would thoroughly nix any idea he might have of keeping her on the down low, by publishing some wedding pics online. And, come to think of it, those pics would also look great on the Beaumont Weddings site. The whole point was that their marriage would not be a secret. By the time she was finished, *everyone* would know, including all of his old flames.

Secondly, Damon needed to learn what it was like to be in a real relationship, one that wasn't based solely on sex. That being the case, one of the things she had to be prepared to do was to say no to sex.

She didn't know how long she could hold out— her track record for saying no to the man was abysmal—but she had to try, because, *four times in their checkered history, if she counted last night,* she had given Damon the prize of sex too soon and too easily.

In the past, the result had been that she had never held him for long: he had always left.

Despite their marriage, she was afraid that if she didn't jolt Damon out of his normal pattern, history would repeat itself and she would never have the warm, loving relationship she wanted.

Thirdly, as part of her relationship strategy, she was going to employ her mother's tactics: she was going to cook. It would be her own special sign of affection. Cooking was something she did for herself, because it reminded her of home. Although she usually dialed back on the traditional meals. Most of her cooking tended toward low-calorie salads and superfoods so she wouldn't put on weight, but she was certain Damon would adjust.

Fourthly, she was going to require wedding rings, for them both.

That was nonnegotiable. They didn't have to be expensive. Hopefully, Damon would show that he cared for her and valued her by getting the rings, which were an important outward sign that they were together.

Feeling more settled and confident by the second, she unbelted her robe, stepped into the shower and switched on the water.

Twenty minutes later, after dressing in jeans and a jersey, she pulled on socks and boots. She dried her hair, wound it up into a knot and quickly did her makeup. A quick spray of perfume and she was good to go.

On cue, Damon stepped through the door, looking broodingly handsome in an oilskin jacket, jeans and the dark gray sweater that clung to his shoulders. His gaze went straight to hers as he shrugged out of the oilskin. "The helicopters will be here in half an hour."

Even though she had already decided that this relationship could not be based on sex alone, she could feel the tantalizing, magnetic pull to spend the thirty minute waiting time in bed with him.

But she was a stronger person than she had been yesterday, so, instead of obeying the urge to walk up to Damon and wrap her arms around his waist, which would definitely lead to sex, she sent him a friendly smile and made a start on her packing then pointedly made the bed.

Just over an hour later, as the two helicopters Damon had hired to transport all of the lodge staff and guests out lifted off, Jenna stared down at the devastation of the storm, which was immediately apparent in the still-swollen river and the leaves and tree branches scattered across the lawn. Thankfully, the lodge itself seemed to have escaped unscathed apart from the broken glass door and some minor damage to the roof.

As the helicopter wheeled, she saw that the bridge was still flooded, and she caught a glimpse of her SUV, looking tiny and forlorn on the side of the road. Apparently Damon had already arranged for repairs and she had already contacted her insurance firm, so now it was just a matter of giving them the garage's details.

After landing at San Antonio, she and Damon boarded a chartered private jet. Happily, because the jet had a number of seats, she didn't have to sit next to him. So, ignoring his level gaze, which had an unsettling, piercing quality and, apparently, the ability to turn her brain off and her body *on*, she sat on the other side of the plane.

She would be able to stick to her program as long as she didn't have to look into his eyes for more than a split second. Opening up her laptop, she immersed herself in work. That wasn't difficult, because she had three weddings in the next week, so she was going to be *busy*.

An hour later, they landed in Houston, which was now mostly sunny, with just a few moody clouds in the sky. After walking down onto the tarmac and collecting their luggage, she informed Damon that she needed to change her clothes.

He gave her one of those remote alpha looks as they stepped into the terminal, as if she'd suddenly just spoken in tongues or landed from Mars, and said, "Why do you need to change? You look fine."

"I look fine for Ransom," she corrected, being careful to avoid direct exposure to his gaze, which had the effect of making her want to take her clothes *off*. "This is Houston. People *know* me here." If she got snapped looking like a refugee from a disaster zone, it would be all over social media sites in seconds.

His brows jerked together. "We'll be in a vehicle in two minutes flat. No one will see you."

She gave him a considering look. "*You* can see me. And it's a fact that you never know who you'll run into at airports." She couldn't count the times she'd crossed paths with someone that she knew or a reporter or blogger who knew her.

Minutes later, she spied a ladies' room. Turning on her heel, she made a beeline for it.

She was almost there when she realized she had forgotten to collect her bag from Damon. She turned and ended up almost colliding with him.

She stepped back, feeling suddenly breathless, because now he had his badass look on, the one that made her want to rip *his* clothes off.

He handed her the bag. "You might need this."

She might need a whole lot of things, but she would take the bag for now.

Once she was in the ladies' room, she found an empty stall and swapped out her jersey and boots, which were now way too hot. The only uncreased piece of daywear she had in her bag was a silky white cotton shirt that sounded cheap but always looked stylish.

Shrugging into the shirt, she buttoned it up over the silk camisole she was wearing, making sure to leave the merest shadow of cleavage.

Just because they weren't having sex for a while didn't mean Damon shouldn't see what he was missing out on.

She slipped on a pair of strappy shoes. Luckily, they were white, so she was coordinated.

Stepping up to the vanity, she freshened her makeup, making sure to give herself sex-goddess eyes, and gave herself another spritz of perfume. Her hair looked good in its tousled knot, so she left it that way. It went without saying that her diamond studs looked perfect.

Collecting her bag and tote, she strolled back out to the concourse and spotted Damon, standing over by a seating area, and, wouldn't you know it, he was talking to a brunette who, even though she had her back to Jenna, looked familiar. Was she psychic or what?

She frowned when the tall, ultraslim brunette flicked her hair in a distinctly flirtatious way that suggested that, if she wasn't a past girlfriend of his, she was trying her hardest to be a future one.

Annoyance humming through her, she noted that Damon running into an attractive, clearly single woman so soon after their wedding underlined the need for rings, for herself, *and for Damon*, because, despite being legally married, there was no visible evidence that he was taken.

The woman half turned and Jenna's stomach sank, because it wasn't one of Damon's numerous exes, or even a future contender. It was Chantal Sanderson, the gossip columnist and blogger to whom she had—anonymously, of course—sent the details of her last fling with Damon.

Dropping her bag beside Damon's on the luggage

cart, she very deliberately linked her arm with his. Ignoring his "what are you up to now" look, she leaned into his side and sent Chantal a bright smile.

Maybe meeting the woman wasn't a complete disaster, because she could think of no better way to telegraph that she and Damon were married than to tell Chantal.

"Hi, I'm Jenna Beaumont," she said smoothly, "Damon's wife. I'm guessing he's just filled you in on our wedding."

After a startled pause, Chantal's glance dropped to Jenna's left hand, which, of course, was bare of rings. Cheeks warming, she resolved to get the ring situation sorted out ASAP.

Chantal, who was now looking like the cat that had gotten the cream, sent her the briefest of polite smiles. "I guess congratulations are in order."

She returned her gaze to Damon. "So… Damon… I didn't know you were even engaged, let alone *married*. Last I heard, and I quote, you would have to be dragged backward through a stampeding herd of cattle before you could be tempted up the aisle. Either that, or someone would have to pay you an extremely large amount of money. And, actually, according to the terms of your uncle's will, isn't that exactly what's just happened?"

Damon's expression was about as immovable as granite. "That would be no comment to both of those."

"Just one more question," Chantal continued smoothly. "Correct me if I'm wrong, but a certain source in the wedding business has it that this isn't even a *real* marriage, that it's more like a forced marriage of convenience?"

Jenna met the gossip columnist's gaze with a steely one of her own. A certain source? Her money was on the florist, Andreas, to whom she might have, unfortunately, confided while they were positioning the wedding arch.

Normally, she would follow Damon's example and say, "No comment," but it occurred to her that Chantal was going to put her own spin on their marriage anyway, so at least she could try to ensure that she got the details right. "To be clear, this is a *real* marriage." If real meant sleeping together and maybe getting pregnant, then, so far, it had been very real. "Damon and I met up again three months ago—"

"So, a whirlwind romance?"

"Not at all," Jenna corrected. "Damon and I have known one another for..." She met his narrowed gaze, tilting her head to one side as if she was having trouble remembering. "How many years—babe?"

Dark amusement surfaced. "I've lost count," he said mildly. "Eight?"

"Closer to ten." She sent Chantal a neutral smile. "We were practically childhood sweethearts—"

Before Jenna could say anything more, Damon pointedly glanced at his watch and jerked his head in the direction of the front doors. "We're late. We need to go."

Moments later, they were moving at pace. "Late for what?"

"Our ride. I left my Jeep with a valet service. They've just pulled up outside in the five-minute parking zone."

Checking behind her, she noted that Chantal didn't seem to be following them. Probably because she had already gotten exactly what she wanted. She glanced at Damon's profile and asked the burning question she hadn't been able to ask in front of the other woman, but which was now making her more and more upset. "Why didn't *you* tell her we were married?"

Damon's response was clipped. "I don't usually share my private life with journalists."

Jenna's heart constricted at Damon's response which, quite frankly, *hurt*, because he had failed to do the one thing she needed him to do in front of Chantal: he had failed to claim her.

Maybe, she shouldn't have expected him to leap to her defense, *as he had when Brad had rung*, or to wrap her close so that they looked loved-up, but she had expected him to at least make some outward show that he was her husband. "Neither do I, but we *are* married, and it's not like people aren't going to find out. Added to that, I'm in the marriage business. That was damage control."

She followed Damon through the glass exit doors and outside into bright daylight. Chest still feeling tight, almost as if she was on the verge of crying, which was absolutely *not* her, she rummaged in her tote for her sunglasses. "And Chantal noticing that there aren't any wedding rings," she muttered huskily, "is exactly why we need them. I know they're not in your marriage rule book, but they're definitely in mine!"

And, in terms of her to-do list, the rings had just shot to number one.

Eleven

Damon slid a pair of sunglasses onto the bridge of his nose.

Despite the confrontation with Chantal and the hurt Jenna hadn't quite been able to hide about the issue of his going public with their marriage, satisfaction curled through him. They were back in Houston, and soon Jenna would be moving into his house and into his bed.

He glanced at Jenna as she strolled with him to the curb. The huge pair of sunglasses hid her expression, but he wasn't fooled: she was still upset, and it was his fault.

His reaction to Chantal, had been kneejerk. He hadn't meant to hurt Jenna by not revealing that they were married. But the damage was done and now he needed to do whatever it took to make it up to her. If that meant buying rings, then he would buy them.

Wedding rings had not been on his list of things to do, since the marriage was just for two months. But, as far as Damon was concerned, they were now a priority.

The thought that Jenna could be pregnant took his breath. The thought of his child growing in her belly set the seal on his possessiveness. After the dysfunction of his childhood, there was no way he would abandon his child.

And if Jenna did turn out to be pregnant, the rings would definitely be required, because, as far as he was concerned, at that point the marriage would be permanent.

Maybe he was jumping the gun with his thinking, but he didn't think Jenna would argue. The way she had responded to Chantal only reinforced that conviction.

In the past, he had spent a great deal of time negating anything that would take him into relationship territory with Jenna. But a car accident and a flooded bridge later—the paralyzing fear that he could have lost her for good—followed by a night of passion, and everything had changed.

He had changed.

He wanted Jenna. And while he didn't know how long he would continue to want her, all he knew for certain was that in ten years, the wanting hadn't stopped.

He didn't think what he felt was romantic love.

There was nothing wishy-washy about the emotions that assailed him. Like the storm that had hit Ransom, what he felt when he looked at Jenna was primitive and intense, his reactions knee-jerk.

The moment she had walked out of the ladies' room was a case in point. All she had done was change her sweater for a white shirt and the boots for high heels, but the transformation had taken her from gorgeous to stunning. It had been all he could do to concentrate on getting clear of Chantal when what he really wanted to do was haul Jenna close and kiss her.

Damon collected his keys from a young man who was standing beside his black Jeep Cherokee. He hadn't told Jenna yet, but since her SUV was stuck in Ransom for the foreseeable future, undergoing repairs, he had phoned ahead and bought another vehicle. His wife was going to need transportation until her SUV was repaired, so he'd had the new SUV delivered to his house.

He was aware that Jenna could react badly to the fact that he had bought her a car. She had been offended by his offer of money to marry him, so giving her the SUV was probably not a good move. But he had bought the vehicle for her anyway, for the simple reason that it had given him pleasure to do so. If she wanted to argue, that was fine.

Oddly, he found himself actually looking forward to the argument.

After loading their luggage in the rear of the Jeep, he held the passenger-side door open for Jenna. As she climbed into the seat, a faint whiff of her perfume teased his nostrils, and he caught another tantalizing glimpse of shadowy cleavage in the silky vee of her shirt—and just like that, every muscle in his body tightened.

Groaning beneath his breath, Damon swung behind the wheel. It was going to be a long afternoon.

On the way to Damon's River Oaks mansion, Jenna asked him to swing by her apartment in uptown Houston so she could collect her things.

But walking into her apartment with Damon in tow was definitely an unsettling experience, because it reminded her of the abrupt way he had ended their relationship so he could marry someone else.

Added to that, the fact that she'd had unprotected sex with him kept popping into her mind, along with the conversation she'd had with Chloe about how on earth she'd managed to get pregnant when she was normally so careful.

Now she knew.

Like her, Chloe had gotten caught up in the passionate, sensual bond that could exist between a man and a woman and had lost every vestige of good sense.

Quite apart from that, the thought that she could be pregnant kept distracting her. She'd been thinking more and more about motherhood, probably because a lot of her friends had young families. Jenna was also a godmother to two gorgeous little bundles, so the idea that a baby could be growing inside her didn't fill her with dismay. If there was a child, she would love it with all her heart, regardless of whether she was with Damon or not.

Stepping into her bathroom, she loaded up on shampoo and conditioner and her favorite shower gel. Just when she thought she had everything, she did a final sweep and realized she had forgotten her body lotion, which was the same sensual fragrance as her perfume, so was therefore indispensable. Duh.

Damon pacing around her small apartment didn't help things. The only times he had been there, they had spent the night together, so of course she kept having multiple flashbacks about that.

When she carried her bags out to the front hall, he was in her sitting room, checking out her family photos, of which she had a *lot*. His absorption with the family portraits brought home the fact that while her life was as transparent as glass, Damon's was largely a mystery to her.

The only photos she had of him were team photos from when he played for the Cougars *and* the few pics she had sneakily shot with her phone.

Damon himself had told her very little about his life. Most of what she did know had been gleaned through town gossip, which was notoriously inaccurate, or personal interaction.

And most of their time together hadn't been normal dating, with long, in-depth conversations. It had involved extreme events—rescues and passionate episodes, which had told her the big things about Damon's character, which she loved, but not the everyday stuff that determined whether or not they were really suited.

It was an aspect of this marriage she hadn't thought too much about, but now she could see the value of the next two months. Finally, they would just be able to spend time together. Saying no to sex was a risk, but if they were to have any chance at a real relationship, sex needed to be paired with actual love.

Looking on edge and distinctly irritable, Damon set down a Christmas photo of her family, complete with silly sweaters and hats. "So, how long have you lived here?"

It was a question about her life that he hadn't been interested in asking during their two-month fling.

"Almost six years," Jenna said breezily as she walked through to her kitchenette, opened the fridge door and started stacking fresh perishables on the bench. If she was going to be gone for two months, no way could she leave yogurt, almond milk and lettuce in her fridge.

Damon surprised her by following her into the kitchen, which was tiny, and leaning against her kitchen counter. She could feel his gaze drilling into her, feel the new curiosity about her life *and* the frustration radiating out from him in waves, because they hadn't made love since last night.

A happy thrill shot through her that her tactic of building a real relationship was already working. What she wasn't prepared for was her own response to having Damon so close. Her body temperature had spiked, and she was actually getting turned on.

*Not helpful. Especially, after the way he had be-
haved at the airport.*

With an effort of will, she stamped out the urge
to give up already, fling herself at Damon and drag
him into the bedroom. Instead, she concentrated on
handing him a cotton shopping bag so he could help
out by loading the perishables.

When she was finished with the fridge, she
checked out the pantry and grabbed a few of her favorite health foods—things that Damon would probably not have, like almonds, pumpkin seeds, quinoa,
chickpeas and dried blueberries. She dropped them
in the bag with the fridge items and, in a neat move,
he turned the tables on her and she found herself
leaning against the counter with his hands landing
on either side of her.

His gaze locked on hers and, suddenly, there was
no air. He dipped his head, his mouth stopping a bare
half inch from hers, giving her the opportunity to
say no if she wanted.

She cupped his jaw and lifted into the kiss. The
pressure of his mouth increased and his hips pinned
her against the counter, sending a shaft of heat
through her.

A split second later, her phone, which was in the
back pocket of her jeans, burst into song. The bland
chiming tune identified it as a work call.

Damon lifted his mouth. "Ignore it," he muttered.

She almost obeyed, but then the real Jenna kicked
in. It occurred to her that a call from anyone right
now was not a bad thing. Not only did it stop her

from making the same mistake she always made with Damon—giving him sex at the drop of a hat—but it would send a message that she had *a life*. "I think I need to get this one."

With grim reluctance, he stepped back.

The caller was her PA. Five minutes later, after she had finally untangled a mix-up with new client appointments, she hung up.

"All done?" Damon asked curtly.

Relieved that the phone call had saved her from tossing her relationship plan and ending up in bed with her irresistibly sexy husband, Jenna picked up her loaded bag of food and followed him out of the kitchen.

Twenty minutes later, with the afternoon sky now clear and the sunset on blast furnace, they turned into the manicured, tree-lined drive to Damon's River Oaks estate.

Jenna had heard of it and, of course, she had googled it, so the Grecian Revival mansion itself was no surprise. Although the gorgeous parklike grounds that stretched to mature trees and the glimpses of the river were. If she needed an expression of Damon's new wealth, this was it.

Damon drove around the side of the house, into a thoroughly modern garage, large enough to house six vehicles, and parked alongside a gleaming silver SUV that looked like the twin of her damaged car.

She climbed out of the Jeep, hooked the strap of her tote over her shoulder, grabbed the bag of perishables and walked around the SUV just to make sure, and discovered she had been wrong.

Not quite a twin, this was the shinier, high-spec, next-generation version. Feeling suddenly suspicious, she eyeballed Damon, who was pulling her suitcase from the rear of the Jeep. "I didn't know you had almost the exact same model SUV as mine."

He closed the trunk. "I don't. I figured you'd need a vehicle while you're waiting for yours to be fixed, so I bought it for you."

Shocked surprise and a warm glow of pleasure flooded Jenna, because Damon had clearly been thinking about her and the things she needed in her life. It was a clear sign that he did value her and wanted to please her.

More than that, she couldn't help thinking that it was exactly the kind of gift an indulgent, *committed* husband who wanted to stay married did buy for his wife.

Her first impulse was to fling her arms around him and give him a huge hug before dancing a happy jig, but then the caution that had hit her after the episode at the airport kicked in.

Damon did seem to be developing real feelings for her, but they weren't there yet. And she couldn't forget that he had offered her money to marry him.

She had been careful to nix any idea that she had designs on his fortune by only allowing him to organize a partner for Beaumont Law. Since she had enabled him to qualify for his inheritance, that had seemed a reasonable exchange. Neither did she feel bad about wanting Damon to pay for wedding rings, since he was the one who required the marriage. But as much as she wanted to accept the expensive new SUV just because he wanted to give it to her, she couldn't, because it could give him the absolute wrong impression about her.

Taking a deep breath, she met his gaze squarely. "The SUV is gorgeous but you'll have to send it back."

He frowned. "I wanted to give you a gift. It's not as if I can't afford it."

"I don't normally take expensive gifts from men—"

"And I'm not exactly a date. I'm your husband."

Damon's blunt statement that he was her husband reignited the glow of pleasure but, until she felt confident that he truly understood she wasn't after his money, she couldn't accept the SUV. "As much as I love it that you bought me a gift," she said carefully, "according to the marriage rules, gift giving is crossing a line." And Damon had been the author of those rules!

"Forget the damn rules." Damon set the bags down. "They were designed for any other woman but you."

Her heart jolted at the admission, which said loud and clear that she was special to Damon, but she had to remind herself that it was not a profession of love.

He linked his fingers with hers and pulled her close, and right there, she began to melt. "That's because you want to have sex with me."

"What's wrong with that?" he growled.

She drew a deep breath. Now was not the time to

give him an admission that she was falling for him, because *that* he was going to have to earn. "We had an agreement for a convenient marriage. I don't want to end up having convenient sex!"

"From where I'm standing, there's nothing convenient about it, and it's not as if we can get in a time machine and go back and *not* have sex."

Damon's words sounded reasonable, and a part of her wanted to agree with him. The only problem was, this was where they came unstuck every time. They went to bed and it was amazing, but in doing so they bypassed real intimacy, because Damon was more than happy to keep his walls up.

Which confirmed that *she* was going to have to be the one to change that pattern, because ten years of being sidelined told her that Damon wasn't going to do it. "I guess not," she said calmly. "But what we can do is slow things down, take a step back—"

"If you don't want to sleep with me," he said coolly, "that's fine. It's always your choice."

A side door into the garage popped open. A middle-aged woman with a comfortable figure and gray-streaked dark hair appeared. The faintly startled look on her face indicated that she had definitely heard the tail end of the conversation.

Voice clipped, Damon introduced Jenna to Consuelo, his housekeeper.

Cheeks warming, she shook Consuelo's hand. Minutes later, still feeling embarrassed, she followed Damon and the older woman through the gorgeous mansion with its dark hardwood floors and jewel-bright rugs. She followed Consuelo up a sweeping staircase. Her suite, which included a sitting room and en suite bathroom, was at the very end of a long hallway.

At a guess, because Chloe had been the original bride, it was as far away from Damon's bedroom as the house allowed. But, now, contrarily, his tacit agreement to the no-sex thing was making her feel that maybe the physical distance wasn't such a positive.

Growing more and more tense by the minute, Jenna tried to appreciate the suite, which was gorgeous and airy, with a large white bed that looked as soft as a cloud. A woven rug softened the dark floor, and a low coffee table situated next to a linen armchair held an enormous vase of pure white roses. Gauzy white curtains filtered the light flooding through tall windows and a gorgeous set of French doors.

The overall impression was distinctly bridal. The roses, in particular, drew Jenna's gaze. She knew she was probably being oversensitive, but she couldn't help thinking that what was clearly a bridal suite had been meant for Chloe, not her. The only time Damon had gotten her roses, they had been a deep, sensual red.

Added to that, the gorgeous room, prepared for another woman, seemed to subtly point out the reality of her relationship with Damon. That, no matter how hard she tried, he saw her more as a sexual partner than a wife.

Consuelo, who had been bustling around the room, opened the French doors and showed Jenna out onto a balcony that overlooked a beautiful parterre garden at the rear of the mansion.

When Jenna stepped back into the bedroom, she saw that Damon had set her suitcase down at the foot of the bed and was in the process of answering a call on his cell. As he lifted the phone to his ear, his gaze connected with hers, informing her that they hadn't finished their conversation. Seconds later, clearly on a business call, he strolled out into the hallway.

One ear tuned to Consuelo's good-natured chatter, the other to Damon's footsteps disappearing down the hallway, Jenna finally allowed herself to relax.

Half an hour later, with her suitcases stowed in the large closet, she sat down and checked work emails then, on impulse, Chantal Sanderson's blog.

Ever since the meeting at the airport, she'd had a feeling that something majorly embarrassing was about to break, and she wasn't wrong. The gossip columnist had taken pictures *and* video of them at the airport and splashed them all over her feed.

And not only that. Seemingly, Murphy's law—*what could go wrong will go wrong*—had struck with a vengeance. As Jenna read Chantal's punch line, she went hot, then cold, then hot again.

Somehow, she had found out that Damon had been rumored to be marrying Chloe but that, clearly, something had gone awry and he had settled for second-choice Jenna instead!

Stomach churning, she closed the page. She

shouldn't let what was gossip get to her, especially not when she had been guilty of fueling the story!

The problem was, it didn't get anywhere close to the truth, that the only reason Damon had married her was that he'd had no choice!

The almost exact opposite reason she had chosen him.

Stepping out onto the balcony, she hugged her arms against the cooler evening air, stared out across the beautiful grounds and tried not to let her mood plummet.

What she needed to remember was that the reason Damon hadn't chosen her as his bride in the first place, and the reason he had constantly walked away from her, wasn't because he didn't feel anything. She was abruptly certain that the truth was the exact opposite: that he felt too much.

Which meant that the only problem she really had was breaking through the walls he'd placed around his heart and getting him to admit it.

Jenna's phone chimed. Frowning, she strolled back into her room and checked the screen, and her stomach sank. It was Brad again! Did that man not have a life? Thankfully, it wasn't a call, just a text.

Her first thought was that he had read Chantal's blog, and she wasn't wrong. The content of his text made her stress levels shoot up another notch.

He would be back in Houston in a few days' time, and he wanted to meet and talk about the partnership proposal.

Feeling distinctly on edge, she quickly texted

back, informing Brad that she'd found a partner, so she wouldn't be sending any proposal.

After taking some time to unpack, she called her PA and checked on messages. She spent a quiet hour catching up on some work on her laptop, checked her watch, then went down to dinner.

It was served in a beautiful dining room and was a collation of hot and cold dishes left by Consuelo on a gleaming antique sideboard so they could serve themselves—grilled steaks and a selection of delicious salads, followed by a raspberry mousse.

Damon strolled in just as she sat down. Clearly, Consuelo hadn't gotten the memo about the separate meal times, or else Damon was transgressing again, because, according to the rules, this was *her* time slot.

Lifting a brow, Damon loaded up his plate and sat directly opposite her, leaving her in no doubt that he was breaking the mealtime rule on purpose.

"Water?" he asked blandly.

When she agreed, he handed her a frosted glass, chinking with ice. She was fairly certain that his fingers *deliberately* brushed hers and, like a switch flicking on, the sensual tension was back.

A little desperately, Jenna decided that she needed to eat quickly and exit the dining room, before she lost the will to hold to her no sex decision. Unfortunately, Damon, who was normally reticent when it came to conversation, now wanted to talk. And, since it was mostly about his arrangements for Beaumont Law, she had to listen.

Not that she retained much of the conversation, because the low, sexy timbre of his voice, made it difficult to concentrate, and she kept getting ensnared in his gaze which were like dark blue tractor beams, blanking her mind for seconds at a time.

By the time they were finished eating, Jenna was definitely hot and bothered, so she set about stacking her plates on the tray Consuelo had left before going home then carrying them through to the kitchen. After rinsing and loading, she closed up the dishwasher.

When she returned to the dining room to grab her phone, thankfully, Damon was on his cell with his briefcase open so, grabbing the reprieve from what had been nothing short of a seduction, she returned to her room.

In order to shift her mind away from hot images of dragging Damon into her bed, she spent the time arranging for a rental car to use in the morning, then moved onto damage control with regard to her marriage.

Maybe she was being too thin-skinned about it, but weddings were her business, and she was going to face a lot of questions from staff and clients, so she needed to put her own story out there.

Luckily, she had pictures of the Vera Wang dress and the cake. She had also taken a lot of photos of the bridal suite and the reception room, so she posted them on her social media sites, along with brief comments to the effect that she *was* married to an old flame.

Feeling exhausted, mostly from fighting her own desire to rush back downstairs and let Damon finish what he had started, she had a quick shower.

She was in her favorite filmy white cotton pajama pants with a matching camisole when there was a knock on her door, and just like that, her pulse rate rocketed.

Because the camisole was just the tiniest bit see through, she opened the door a crack. Damon was leaning against the doorjamb, his shirt undone at the throat, his hair sexily ruffled, as if he'd been running his fingers through it.

He lifted a brow. "Do you want to continue on where we left off?"

With seduction.

Her breath stalled in her throat. "Are you talking about the conversation, or…?"

There was a vibrating silence. He shrugged. "I know we need to talk," he said in a gruff voice. "It's not exactly my strong suit, but…it's your choice."

She didn't know if it was being given a choice that melted her insides or if it was just that she couldn't resist Damon—all she knew was that it felt like it had been a long time since she'd been in his arms, and when she was in his arms, the negatives seemed to dissolve.

Despite all the angst and stress around their relationship, suddenly, she definitely didn't want to talk.

Opening the door, she took a half step toward him, ran her palms up and over his chest, curled her fingers into the lapels of his shirt, and pulled him into her room. "Just one more night…then we go by the rule book."

Amusement surfaced in Damon's gaze and his mouth quirked, suddenly making him look crazy sexy. "I know what I'd like to do with the rule book," he growled.

Closing the door behind him, he bent to capture her mouth.

Winding her arms around his neck, she went up on her toes. The hungry pressure of his kiss sent a raw shudder through her. She knew she should resist, and she would.

Tomorrow.

While Damon was busy kissing her, she multitasked by unbuttoning his shirt and peeling it from his shoulders. Her breath came in as the golden wash of light from the setting sun flared over taut bronzed muscles. She found his zipper and dragged it down before Damon's hand halted her progress.

"This time," he muttered, "we take it slow."

Another kiss and a few slow steps backward and they reached her bed.

Heat surged through her as Damon disposed of her camisole. His mouth brushing her shoulder sent another sensual throb through her. A split second later her pajama pants floated to the floor and she was naked.

A wave of melting heat flowed through her as Damon cupped her breasts and bent to take one in his mouth. For long, tense moments she lost focus as the ache low in her belly coiled tight. Just when she thought she couldn't take any more, he peeled out of his pants then lifted her into his arms.

Her breath came in as he deposited her on the bed, and sprawled beside her then her brain snapped into gear when she realized how close they were to making love. "Please tell me you've got a condom."

With a flashing grin, he reached for his discarded pants and delved into the pocket. "While you were in the bathroom at the airport, I bought a whole box."

She stared, riveted, as he produced several foil packets of varying colors and textures and tumbled them into her hands.

"And I was hoping that you would do the honors..."

Twelve

Four days later Damon woke at six after another restless night alone. Jenna had given him a long relationship talk, and he had listened. Apparently, he sucked at communication, and his gift-giving ratio was right up there with flying pigs: nonexistent. But transitioning from an alpha to a beta wasn't going to be easy.

Additionally, he ate too much meat which, apparently, gave him hypertension. Betas ate quinoa and blueberries and possessed emotional intelligence. They were nicer and lived longer, so he needed to get onboard.

He was trying.

Tossing the bedcovers aside, he paced to the French doors that opened onto the patio and stepped out, the morning air cool against his naked chest.

He stared across the sweeping lawns, bounded by the mature oaks that enclosed that end of the property, and at the glimpse of the parterre garden that Consuelo's husband, Jack, kept in perfect order.

The veranda ran around the house, giving outside access to all six upstairs suites. Jenna's room was around the corner from his, at the back of the house. As tempted as he was to stroll around there, he knew better than to do so.

His wife wanted some time. Given that she had agreed to marry him when he'd been on the verge of losing his inheritance, and that his desire for her had been unruly enough that he could have made her pregnant, he was honor bound to give her all the time she needed.

Unfortunately, that didn't stop him from wanting her. And, after ten years, he was fast reaching the conclusion that there was no silver bullet for the intense desire that had hit him like a kick from a mule when Jenna had sashayed out onto the Cougars' practice field in tight pink Lycra.

He gripped the damp balustrade in the hope that the cool wood would dampen down the heat that burned through him. If there was one thing he had learned about Jenna lately, pushing didn't work. When she set her mind to something, changing it was like turning the *Titanic*.

As frustrating as that trait was, it was a quality that drew him to her. If she'd been less strong, he would have been bored within minutes. But, after four days of living with her in the same house, without her in his bed, he was close to breaking point.

Broodingly, he considered that it was probably just as well that Jenna left for work early and insisted on filling any spare time in the evenings by producing healthy vegan dishes that, apparently, he needed because his system was choking on grilled steaks and if he didn't eat some of her food, he would *die*.

Jaw taut, he returned to his room and decided to burn off some of his frustration by going for a run. An hour later, he returned to the house, had a shower and dressed for work.

He walked downstairs at seven thirty, but any plans to catch a few stolen minutes with Jenna were scuttled when he reached the kitchen just in time for her to place a plate of chia seed and blueberry pancakes with coconut yogurt in front of him.

Gifting him a beaming smile and a "'Bye, babe!" she strolled out the side door to the garage, looking gorgeous in a pale blue linen dress that clung to her figure, sexy four-inch heels, her hair piled up in a loose knot with tendrils curling around her nape.

Frowning, he considered that Jenna's breezy, positive manner wasn't just a time-out because she wanted to generate a real relationship between them, but actually signaled that she was cooling off and didn't want him anymore.

The second he considered that option, he discarded it. He might be transitioning into a beta, but he still had some alpha instincts.

Four nights ago the passion had been white-hot

and instant. There was no way Jenna could have faked that.

He mulled over possible reasons for the change.

He knew for a fact that Jenna wasn't worried about Beaumont Law anymore, because the new senior partner was already installed. It had cost him a small fortune, a fact he wouldn't disclose to her, but the guy he had gotten was top-notch and trustworthy, so she wouldn't have to worry about her family firm again.

He didn't think she was upset about having to move out of her apartment for two months. Although neither of them was used to actually living with anybody else—

He went still at that thought and wondered why he hadn't considered that aspect of Jenna before. She was drop-dead gorgeous and a catch. He had lost count of the number of men who had pursued her, but the fact remained that, like him, Jenna had remained single; she had never actually had a live-in relationship.

While he drank coffee and munched his way through the blueberry pancakes—which, with a heavy pour of maple syrup (not on the diet) and some of the whipped cream he'd hidden in the meat bin in the fridge, were actually okay—he checked Chantal Sanderson's feed.

She had written inflammatory pieces about him before, a mixture of fiction and downright lies that indicated she should be writing novels rather than digging into the lives of innocent people, so he didn't expect to read anything uplifting.

He wasn't wrong. Sanderson made him look like a cross between Buffalo Bill and the devil, but what really ticked him off was the sister wives comment and the crack she had made about Jenna being his second choice.

Hands down, from the moment she had winked at him, she had been his first choice.

He checked the time and, on impulse, called Caleb before he left for the office.

Caleb's voice when he answered the call was curt. "I'll be late into the office this morning," he muttered. "Chloe's got morning sickness."

Damon's fingers tightened on the phone. "I heard you and Chloe were expecting a baby. Congratulations, by the way."

"Thanks," Caleb muttered. "Sorry I didn't tell you earlier, but finding out she was pregnant was a game changer."

And just like that, Damon's chest banded tight. He had pushed the thought that Jenna could be pregnant to the back of his mind, because it filled him with an odd pastiche of emotions, including fierce possessiveness and a gut-wrenching fear that he would not make a good father.

He grasped for something to say on a subject he knew little about. "How far along is she?"

Caleb lowered his voice, as if he didn't want Chloe to hear. "Do we have to talk about the pregnancy?" he muttered. "Chloe goes a little crazy when that happens."

"Because of the morning sickness?"

There was the sound of hurried footsteps and a door closing, as if Caleb had moved into a different room. "There's a list of things that make her crazy," he said in a more normal voice. "The fact that I got her pregnant in the first place, then the subject we're not allowed to talk about, aka, I ditched her. Then there's the issue that we're not married and, finally, that we *are* getting married. And there's one more that I almost forgot. I haven't gotten Chloe an engagement ring, and apparently that means I *definitely* don't love her."

Damon checked his watch. He had a sudden urge to get in the Jeep and drive for a long time. "Sounds like you've got a lot on your plate."

"We're getting the rings today," the other man said, sounding hunted. "Wedding *and* engagement, and if there's a rock there the size of Texas, apparently that's the one I have to buy, because it's my fault she's pregnant."

Damon frowned. "Is an engagement ring that important?"

"I want to get her a ring, of course I do. I love her," Caleb said flatly. "But, if you don't get the ring, apparently that means you're not generous, and you don't love them…and that means *no sex*."

Damon drove out of his driveway and accelerated into traffic.

He had never seen Caleb, who was the strong, silent type, as a love doctor, but he was fast changing his mind.

Jenna had made a point of saying she wanted a wedding ring, so he would damn well make sure she had that. In the past, he hadn't given her gifts, because that would have signaled the relationship he had been at pains to avoid, but now things were different. They were married—even if only temporarily—and it was a fact that Jenna had to deal with people like Chantal Sanderson, who had publicly noted that Jenna did not wear either a wedding or an engagement ring.

That being the case, he would make sure Jenna also had an engagement ring, and that she was very publicly showered with gifts that would send a clear message to anyone interested that no way was she second best.

Although he had no clue how he was going to achieve getting an engagement ring on her finger when she had refused the SUV.

Twenty minutes later, Damon strolled into his Houston office. First up, he called Hennessey to check up on the lodge repairs and the state of the bridge. He was just about to hang up when his lodge manager said something that destroyed his beta mode.

"I forgot to tell you earlier that that lawyer that used to live in Ransom called a few days ago, trying to get hold of Jenna. Apparently, he couldn't get her on her cell, so that was probably when you were on your flight. Just thought you should know."

Jaw tight that Brad Henderson was still calling Jenna, Damon thanked him and hung up.

His next call was to a longtime friend from Ransom who now ran his own detective agency in Houston. The first attempt went to voice mail. Damon was about to terminate the second call when Nick Duval finally picked up.

As soon as he mentioned Henderson's name, Nick tagged him. "That's the lawyer who used to work for Beaumont Law?"

"That's him. He walked away from his partnership in Houston about a month ago and has been in LA for the past couple of weeks."

"Let me guess. He's been back in touch with Jenna. And, by the way," he said hastily, "I saw online that you were married, so I guess congratulations are in order."

"Which is why I want you to check him out. Years ago he had something of a reputation—"

"With women—usually married women."

"There were also rumors he was involved in some kind of hedge fund deal that went sideways."

"Oh, yeah…scamming the retired people." There was a tapping sound, as if Nick was using his laptop. "Henderson comes from *big* money. Apparently, his father's a wealthy developer in California, so none of that surprises me. How soon do you need the report?"

"Yesterday."

"I'll get back to you as soon as I can, but if I'm checking out what he's up to in LA, it might take a few days. I've got a guy out there. He's good. If you want, I can get him to tail Henderson. That's going to be the most efficient way to investigate."

"Do whatever you have to." After giving Nick his email address, Damon hung up.

The fact that Brad Henderson was still in the mix made Damon frown. He'd been in the background of Jenna's life for years, even though she had never gotten involved in an actual relationship with him.

And that would happen now over his dead body.

Jenna walked into her office later that afternoon to find several extremely expensive bunches of roses from a prestigious florist occupying almost every spare surface. And they were not ordinary roses. She had ordered and arranged enough of them to recognize that these were the premium, *scented* roses, the kind that cost a small fortune.

She found a card and turned it over. The simple message—*from Damon*—made her heart skip a beat.

Eyes misting just a little, because, other than the SUV, and the bunch of red roses he had sent her a few weeks ago—and which didn't count, because they had been his slightly more upmarket way of ditching her—this was the first *valid* gift Damon had ever given her.

She checked all the cards, seven of them in total, all bearing the same message. And she recognized the signature. The cards were handwritten by Damon, which meant he had actually gone to the florist, not simply gotten his PA to order them.

Her chest banded tight at the thought. She sniffed

and rummaged in her tote for a tissue, which was a little ridiculous but, lately, she seemed to be more emotional than usual.

As gorgeous as the roses were, as much as they made her melt inside, she knew she should tread carefully. Damon had behaved well over the last four days, and they had even had some actual conversations, but she couldn't help but be aware that he was frustrated that they weren't sleeping together.

It was there in the faint abruptness she detected when she went to bed and in his gruff manner in the morning when he tried to get the extremely complicated coffee machine to work.

She bent and inhaled the heavenly rose scent and any doubts flew out the window. Damon was making a genuine effort, and she couldn't help loving that he had sent her such a thoughtful and romantic gift.

One of her senior wedding planners, and a good friend, Megan, popped her head around her door. "Ooh, you've found them. That's so sweet." She waggled her brows. "I'm guessing they're from your new husband?"

For a moment, her mind went blank, because the word *husband* and Damon hadn't quite come together in her mind, then a small rush of pleasure replaced the blankness. "Yes. Damon sent them."

Megan crossed her arms over her chest. "I wish Gerald would give me flowers."

Jenna blew her nose, which was suddenly running like a tap, but at least she wasn't crying. It occurred to her that it could be premenstrual tension, because she had almost flown into a rage when her latest bride had decided to have *three* changes of wedding gowns, which would mean she would have to assign a second assistant to help with the designer and the fittings. "We're still in the honeymoon stage," she said a little breathlessly, because suddenly that was how it was beginning to feel.

"I remember that phase," Megan said wistfully. "Although, three kids later, it seems like a long time ago."

Jenna's phone chimed. Picking it up, she checked the screen. It was Damon, and just like that she felt as giddy as a teenager.

He was brief. He had a gap in his schedule, and he wanted to get wedding rings. Could she meet him outside in an hour?

Jenna retrieved her planner and flicked through pages. "As it happens, I'm free in an hour, so I'll see you downstairs then."

There was a small silence. "Babe, did you get my flowers?"

"Yes, I did, and I *love* them," she said, not bothering to hide how emotional she felt. "Thank you so much. I don't think anyone's ever given me so many."

"I got all of them," Damon said bluntly.

And out of nowhere, her heart soared.

Suddenly, the love relationship with Damon that she wanted seemed entirely possible.

Thirteen

Damon made sure to get to Jenna's building early enough that he had time to cruise around and find a parking space.

When she appeared, looking as stunning as she had when she'd placed the plate of perfectly made pancakes in front of him that morning, predictably, his pulse rate accelerated. Climbing out of the driver's seat, he walked around and opened her door.

She flashed him a smile as she climbed into the passenger side seat of his Jeep. As she did so, her already short dress hiked up, showing off even more of her long, tanned legs.

Groaning beneath his breath, Damon swung behind the wheel, pulled into traffic and willed his arousal to subside. That was the dangerous alpha tendency. He was trying to behave, but it was going to be a long afternoon.

With her seat belt fastened and her tote positioned at her feet, Jenna instantly disappeared into her phone. She scribbled a note on a small pad she extracted from her bag and handed it to him. "This is the name of a reputable jeweler who'll give us a good deal on rings."

Damon braked for lights and checked out the address, which began with the word *Budget*. It didn't sound like the kind of store from which Caleb would be purchasing Chloe's engagement ring.

And at a guess, it wouldn't stock the designer brands that Jenna usually wore, either, which suggested that she expected him to be cheap when it came to the rings.

As if he was still stuck in the past and couldn't afford to buy her anything expensive.

With careful precision, he placed the address in the console between the seats and accelerated smoothly through the intersection. They could visit the budget jewelry store if Jenna wanted, but he already knew where he wanted to shop.

He wanted the best for her so that it was clear that she *was* his *first* choice. More than that, he wanted to make up for the hurts of the past, and all the times he should have gotten her a gift and hadn't, so it would be a cold day in hell before he put a cheap ring on her finger.

Twenty minutes later, he pulled into the underground garage of a major mall and turned his head.

The last few minutes of the drive had been quiet, mostly because Jenna had gone to sleep, which he found oddly endearing, because for the first fifteen minutes she had been busy either checking her phone, reading online articles or making lists. If there was an unutilized moment, he had missed it.

Her head was presently turned toward him, her lashes ridiculously long, dark crescents against her flushed cheeks. Tendrils of blond hair fell silkily around her neck, and her mouth was soft.

Her eyes flickered, and for a split second he found himself staring into blue eyes with velvety dark centers, the irises shot through with intriguing silver striations. For a long moment, her expression was dazed, and her gaze clung to his.

With an effort of will, Damon controlled the urge to lean down and kiss her, which was just as well, because almost immediately she blinked and straightened. "We're here. Good." Briskly, she unfastened her seat belt and picked up her tote. "Let's get this done."

It was not, exactly, the most romantic start to what he hoped would be a turning point in their relationship. A relationship that, until the last few days, he had avoided, because every time he looked at Jenna, he was shunted into his past.

A past he preferred to forget, and which had taught him that women like Jenna didn't stay long term with men like him.

Jenna smothered a yawn as she looked around at the huge downtown parking garage. She still felt weirdly exhausted, and it wasn't like her to fall asleep during the day. Normally when she woke up at six in the morning, she was instantly wired and didn't stop until she dropped into a deep sleep at night. "Where are we?"

"The Atraeus Mall. I thought we'd go shopping for rings here first."

She climbed out of the Jeep and slung the strap of her tote over her shoulder as Damon joined her. "What about the budget store?"

"If you want to buy jewelry from there," he said carefully, "we can go there next, but I'd like to start shopping here."

She gave him a patient look. "I don't *like* the budget jewelry—no one does—but the ring is only for two months—"

"Unless you're pregnant—" He stopped himself right there. "They're just rings," he said mildly, "and since I needed the marriage, I'm buying."

She blinked, as if she was still trying to digest the switch from alpha to beta, then smiled. "It's just wedding bands, so, okay. Where are we shopping?"

Damon pressed the Jeep's key lock. "I've arranged to get the rings from Ambrosi."

She stared at him for a long moment, then fell into step with him. "Ambrosi's *expensive*."

"I read Chantal's blog. Damned if I'll get you anything cheap."

Warmed by the protective note in Damon's voice, which utterly derailed her from the question of expensive rings, Jenna caught their reflections in the glass of the doors that opened into the exclusive Atraeus Mall. Damon was broad and muscular and totally sexy in his dark suit, edgy white linen shirt and cobalt-blue tie. Even though she was wearing four-inch heels, he somehow managed to make her look small and fragile, when usually, with shoes on, she was the same height as most men she dated.

Happily, since he'd sprung Ambrosi on her, her white linen dress and the expensive glitter of her trusty Chanel earrings and matching diamond bracelet were upscale enough to shop there.

A leisurely stroll through the busy mall, filled with shoppers carrying designer bags or sitting at the cafés interspersed with the designer boutiques, and they reached the signature white-and-gilt Ambrosi store. They were met by the manager, Bruno Casale, who instantly recognized Jenna because she regularly brought him clients to shop for rings and other wedding jewelry.

Chatting smoothly and oozing charm, he showed them through to a private room, with beautiful leather couches, soft rugs and glowing antique furniture. Jenna sat down. Damon seated himself beside her, close enough that she could feel the heat of his body and smell the subtle masculine scents of soap and cologne. The warmth of his thigh brushed hers, and a heady awareness hummed through her.

A pretty redhead, Ellen, brought in a tray of champagne and chilled water, with the appropriate glasses, which signaled that Damon hadn't just asked for the room; he was paying the exorbitant cost of a genuine, over-the-top private appointment.

Feeling suddenly crazily happy, but a little on edge, because she just hadn't expected Damon to do anything like this, she watched Ellen pour the champagne, which was French and vintage. With practiced movements, she positioned the half-filled flutes and the tall, frosted glasses of water within easy reach.

The door popped open again, and Bruno returned, wheeling a familiar cart, which had multiple drawers containing black velvet trays of jewelry. With careful precision, he placed trays, not of wedding rings, but *engagement* rings on the coffee table. And they were not small rings.

Ambrosi, who were known for the exquisite quality of their pearls and diamonds, had tiered collections. The pretty, less expensive pieces were on display in the shop; a few of the more expensive pieces were, too, but the astronomical stuff sat in the vault and only made an appearance in the private appointments, or in online catalogs that the rich and famous perused.

This was the rich and famous collection.

When Bruno turned away to get further trays of jewelry, Jenna turned to Damon. Her heart was pounding. The roses had made her emotional, but *this* was making her feel almost panicked. This morning when she'd left the house, she'd had all her ducks in a row. Her campaign to restart their relationship had been progressing nicely, but now she felt as if she'd lost her bearings.

She liked diamonds, and she loved the diamond jewelry that had been given to her over the years by her family to celebrate special occasions, because it meant something to her, and that was the point. She didn't know why Damon wanted to give her an engagement ring.

And some of the rings Bruno was producing were on a whole other level. They were investment pieces, the kind of jewelry wealthy people sank their money into, much as they might buy stocks and shares. The kind of jewelry that was regarded as money in the bank.

And that wealthy husbands bought for their wives.

"I thought we were just getting wedding bands."

His gaze connected with hers. "If we're getting the bands, then we may as well get the engagement ring, too."

Before she could answer, Bruno slid more trays on the table, some containing actual sets of jewelry, including earrings, bracelets and pendants. It was too much. "Bruno," she said a little huskily. "We need to discuss a couple of things. Do you mind if we step outside for a few minutes?"

Like the consummate professional he was, Bruno was unfazed. "Of course." He opened a second door that led into another room. "Please…use my office. It's more private."

Damon followed her into Bruno's office. Closing the door behind him, he said quietly, "What's the problem?"

She met his gaze squarely. "We never agreed on an engagement ring."

"You said you wanted a wedding ring, and for people to know that the marriage was real. What better way than to also have an engagement ring? It's what most women have."

She drew a deep breath and tried to marshal her thoughts, which was difficult with Damon looking muscular, sexy, and *GQ* perfect. "I wanted a wedding ring because I've been brought up to expect to have one. Plus, I work in the wedding business, so my staff and clients will expect me to wear a ring. If I don't, they'll be asking who abducted the real Jenna. And I want *you* to wear a ring because it makes it clear that you're married, and that means I don't have to spend the next two months batting off women who think they can get you—"

"Which is exactly the reason I want you to have an engagement ring," he stated flatly. "Because if Henderson or any other guy comes sniffing around, the rings spell out that you belong to me and that, if they even think of trying anything, they will be dealing with me."

Damon was claiming her, *again*, his words blunt, declarative and definitively alpha. Despite the fact that there was nothing PC about them, they sent a sharp electrical thrill down Jenna's spine.

It wasn't a declaration of love, not even close. It was more about the possessive kind of burning jealousy she knew just a little too much about, the kind that had kept her up nights. But it meant that she *mattered* to Damon, and out of nowhere her heart soared again, because maybe, just maybe, he was finally on the edge of falling for her.

Letting out a shaky breath, because now she definitely did feel emotional, she lifted her chin. "Okay."

There was a moment of silence. "Okay, what?" he said warily.

"You can get me the engagement ring."

"You won't argue if I want to get a big one?"

She sniffed and realized she needed a tissue again. What was *wrong* with her? "I won't argue."

"Good," he muttered, then pulled her close and kissed her.

When Damon released her, Jenna worked hard to suppress the bubble of joy that threatened to burst and shimmer right through her. She had to keep reminding herself that Damon wanting her to wear his ring on her finger wasn't a declaration of love.

But it was the closest thing she'd had so far.

Feeling flushed and still a little emotional, she took her seat in front of the glittering trays of rings.

She noticed that a tray of salmon canapés had been deposited beside the champagne. The smell of the fish hit her nostrils and a hot, nauseous feeling rose up in her, then subsided into a general feeling of unease.

The sudden thought that she could be pregnant froze her in place.

With the stress of the last few days, she had

thought about the possibility, but because it was way too early to tell, and she was still expecting her period, she had pushed the idea to the back of her mind. But now she had to seriously consider the notion. And, in her family, pregnancies were cataclysmic.

According to her mother, she had started out suffering mood swings and cravings, then she'd had morning sickness bad—think zombie, for weeks— which was why she had waited eight years to have Luke. Jenna's aunt Victoria hadn't had the mood swings, she'd just had the cravings, about forty pounds' worth that had then taken two years to lose.

She seemed to remember her mother saying that she had *known*, like, on the night. Jenna didn't think she had that kind of mystic connection with her womb—she would be relying on a test kit—but she was definitely feeling…different.

Bruno placed a tray of wedding rings on the table, but Jenna ignored them and gave the store manager a chiding look, because he should know better. There was no point deciding on the wedding rings until she had chosen an engagement ring, because the wedding rings needed to match.

Bypassing the champagne, she reached for a chilled glass of water, because if she was pregnant she shouldn't drink any alcohol. Taking a sip, she placed the glass down and began perusing the trays of diamond rings.

She knew what she liked; she was a solitaire girl all the way. She started small, sliding on one glittering ring after another, until she had almost made up her mind. She was just about to suggest that the ring she had on was it when Damon reached for a tray she had consciously avoided, because it was the crazy expensive tray, which contained just half a dozen rings, each one of them with extra-large diamonds of varying colors and cuts.

He picked out a pure white pear-shaped diamond that shot out streamers of fire. "You should try this one."

Feeling like she might have been sipping champagne instead of the water, Jenna slipped off the pretty solitaire, placed it carefully back in its tray and held out her hand for the ring Damon was holding. Instead of letting her take it, he turned her hand over and gently but firmly slid the ring onto the third finger of her left hand.

The deliberate way he placed the ring on her finger spun her back to their wedding vows and to the disappointment that had swamped her when there was no ring. She realized that, in his own way, he was trying to make up for that oversight, and in that moment something broke open inside her, a core of hurt she thought she had dealt with but which she clearly hadn't.

Taking a deep breath, she met his gaze, and for long seconds the room dissolved. Blinking, she looked at the elegant, exquisite ring on her hand, which looked…perfect. She didn't want to sabotage what was happening between them, to read too much into Damon's actions, but, right there and then, they had definitely had a moment, and despite her caution, hope spiraled inside her.

Because she was in love with Damon. Completely, irrevocably.

And that meant that the stakes were now higher than ever, because she no longer wanted to walk away, and she didn't just want Damon to love her—she needed him to do so.

He turned her hand so that the afternoon sunlight streaming through the windows made the beautiful diamond glitter and shine. "The shape of that diamond suits your hand." His gaze locked with hers. "If you like it, we'll take it."

There was no question. "I love it," Jenna said simply.

How could she not when, like the roses, this was a gift of love, even if Damon didn't quite know it yet.

A warm flood of pleasure infused her. She could hardly believe they had come so far, so quickly, or that it was looking like Damon was, finally, falling head over heels in love with her.

Fourteen

The next three days were insanely busy at work. Added to that, Damon had had to go away for a night, so it was easy to stick to her plan and avoid intimacy. On the morning of the day he was supposed to get back, Jenna went to work as usual and raced through a number of meetings, mostly because she had a session with an extremely wealthy bride and groom at Ambrosi, and the appointments tended to go long.

This time the Ambrosi session made her unexpectedly emotional, because she kept catching glimpses of the gorgeous engagement ring and the sleek matching wedding band on her finger and reliving the moment they'd had. Added to that, although Damon was just away for the one night, she was *missing* him.

Even though they hadn't been sleeping together, she had gotten used to living in his house, and to Damon's presence. She had expected him to be bad-tempered about the no-sex rule, and he had been initially but, lately, they had settled into a comfortable routine. The night before he had left, Damon had even cooked for her. It had been Tex-Mex, with no quinoa in sight, but he'd included plenty of salad to please her and, she had to admit, it had been delicious.

Jenna's phone chimed, so she checked her messages, happy anticipation making her mood soar because it was probably Damon texting her, since he was due back that afternoon.

It wasn't Damon; it was Brad.

Instantly, the warm feeling evaporated, to be replaced by irritation, since he knew the Beaumont Law deal was off. But for some reason, he had still come to Houston and was insisting that she see him anyway.

Annoyed, she agreed to meet him for a few minutes, but only because he had been prepared to help her out with Beaumont Law when she'd been desperate. The place he wanted to meet was the jeweler Tiffany's at the Galleria Mall, which wasn't that far from her office. Happily, it was later on in the afternoon when she had no appointments, so it wasn't too inconvenient.

Bruno's redheaded assistant offered Jenna a glass of champagne. Absently, she took it, even though she had no intention of drinking. The fumes of the vintage champagne, which were normally floral and light, rose to her nostrils and, out of the blue, her stomach reacted. Setting the glass down, she pushed to her feet, excused herself and rushed to the bathroom.

By the time she got there, the nauseous feeling had subsided, but she was perspiring and still felt slightly off. She ran cold water over her wrists for a few moments then, using a dampened hand towel, dabbed at her face to freshen up

She stared at herself in the mirror. That was the second time that had happened, and she hadn't had her period, which should have happened yesterday at the latest.

She was almost certain she was pregnant.

Feeling over the moon, but also shocked and unsettled because, after years of wallowing in limbo with relationships, suddenly she was married and, maybe, pregnant, she went back to her wealthy clients and tried to look calm and interested in their lives.

A torturous hour later, her bride and groom finished drinking champagne and choosing astronomically priced jewelry. Sliding her cell back in her tote, Jenna strolled out of Ambrosi and looked for a pharmacy.

A few minutes later, after speaking with one of the assistants, she purchased a pregnancy test. Apparently, because she was more than a week on from possible conception, *and* her period hadn't appeared, she should get a result.

Feeling too on edge to take the test in a public

restroom, she collected her rental and drove to River Oaks, which, in light traffic, was just a few minutes away. Waving at Consuelo, who was busy polishing furniture, she walked up to her room and into the bathroom.

Minutes later, she had the result.

Holding the stick in one hand as if it was a bomb about to explode, she sat down on the edge of the bath. She could go to her doctor and get her to do a test, just to confirm, but she didn't need to, because she *knew*.

She was pregnant.

Taking a deep breath, she laid her hand on her stomach. It didn't feel any different, but her breasts did; they were definitely more sensitive.

Dropping the stick back in the packet, she tossed it in the trash and washed her hands. After drinking a glass of water, she walked back downstairs, got into her SUV and drove back to work.

She was almost there when she remembered that she was supposed to meet Brad. If she went now she would be way early, but it didn't make sense to go to the office then turn around and drive to the mall he had mentioned, so she made the decision to go straight there.

Taking a left turn, she headed for The Galleria. Fifteen minutes later, she walked through to the main concourse and eventually found Tiffany's, which was another gorgeous jewelry store, popular with her clients. She briefly wondered why on earth Brad wanted to meet there but decided that maybe it was because the store was iconic and easy to find.

After waiting outside for a while, she decided to kill some time strolling along the shop fronts. It was her fault she was early, but even so, she couldn't help feeling impatient that she had to wait for Brad when all she wanted to do was check in at the office then go home. And she would be in a hurry on the way home, because she needed to shop for ingredients for the new dish she had planned to cook for Damon tonight.

Once they had eaten, she would tell him about the baby, then they would have to have a serious talk about the future, because now it wasn't just about them; it was also about their child.

Jenna paused in front of a baby shop and, on impulse, walked in. She picked up a tiny, stretchy little suit designed for a newborn and smoothed her fingers over the soft material. Setting that down, she picked up a tiny set of knitted booties.

She didn't know how Damon would react to fatherhood, but she was almost certain he would take to it like a duck to water because, for all his toughness, he was a natural protector.

Her stomach tightened and a sharp electrical tingle shimmered through her at the thought of Damon in warrior mode. Once he knew she was pregnant, with his alpha instincts, she was almost certain he would not want to end their marriage. He would want to keep her close, and maybe, just maybe, he would finally tell her what she needed to hear—that he loved her.

* * *

Damon checked his phone when he got off his flight. There were no work calls, which suited him, because his plan was to drive straight home. Normally he would call in at the office, but right now he found himself more interested in whether or not Jenna would be working late and what superfood concoction she would insist on cooking for dinner.

He was about to call her, but Nick had phoned him a couple of times, so he hit his number first.

He picked up almost immediately. Nick didn't have the information on Henderson yet but was expecting it soon. He just wanted to give Damon a heads-up that the PI he had put on Henderson had just called to say that the man had flown into Houston and had made an arrangement to meet with Jenna. The PI, Jeff Soames, had caught the same flight and was still tailing Henderson. Nick gave him Soamse's cell phone number and the meeting place in the Galleria.

He also had one more piece of information to impart. Apparently, Henderson had political aspirations, and he had let it drop to a few movers and shakers that he'd been making plans to take over Beaumont Law, marry Jenna and use that connection to run for office in Texas.

Damon's jaw compressed. Beaumont Law was no longer on the table and Jenna was married to him for two months, which left one possibility—that Henderson was angling for a future marriage with Jenna. *Once Damon was out of the picture.*

He didn't want to believe any of it after the past few days with Jenna, but Henderson had continued to phone her and was now meeting her. None of it jelled with Jenna's plan for them to try for a real relationship. None of it jelled with his gut, but it was a fact she was no longer in his bed, and the meeting just happened to be at an expensive jeweler's. There could only be one reason for that: Henderson was buying her something.

Probably an engagement ring.

Stomach tight, Damon called his office and canceled his appointments, then he called Soames. Henderson was en route to the mall, with an ETA of fifteen minutes. Twenty minutes later, Damon left the Jeep in the parking garage of the Galleria and walked through the busy mall.

Jenna checked her watch, her foot tapping as she waited for Brad.

When she finally spotted him, she was almost on the point of leaving.

His gaze went straight to her rings. "I heard that you married Wyatt and that he's put one of his lawyers into Beaumont Law."

Jenna stiffened. "It's not exactly a secret."

"But it is a shame, since *I* was hoping to marry you. I still am."

Her brows jerked together. Marry Brad? She would sooner jump off the Pleasant River Bridge. "Then you should forget about it, because it's never going to happen."

"But you know your parents wanted it," he said, impatiently. "Why do you think I hung around Beaumont Law? It was for you." He glanced around, almost as if he was nervous. "You know I've always had political aspirations. My focus is on running for governor in Texas in the next election, but it all swings on being married to you."

And she finally got it. "Because my father was governor for three terms."

"I've got the money. You bring the pedigree."

And, suddenly, Brad made perfect sense. "It's still never going to happen," she said flatly. "I'm married to Damon, and I intend to stay married to him."

Brad gave her a long look then jerked his head in the direction of a nondescript, medium-height guy in a sports jacket, who was holding up his phone, as if he was reading something. "See that guy over there? He's tailed me from LA. I got my people to check him out, and he's been hired by Wyatt to watch me, because guess what? Your husband thinks we're having an affair."

Brad looked over her right shoulder for a long, vibrating second before abruptly walking away.

A curious tension running up her spine, Jenna turned. When she saw Damon just steps away and approaching fast, her stomach sank. She knew he had been annoyed that Brad had been calling her, so he would hate it that she'd arranged to meet him, even if it was just to tell him to leave her alone. "Damon—"

His gaze locked with hers, stopping the words in her throat. Instead of asking her what was going on, he strode over to the guy Brad had pointed out and started talking to him, and Jenna went still inside. She hadn't believed Brad when he'd said that Damon was having them both investigated because he thought they were having an affair, but now she did.

Too late to wish she hadn't played the jealousy card with Brad, because it now looked like Damon actually believed she was two-timing him!

He finally came back to her, his gaze cool. "Soames said Henderson arranged to meet you here."

Jenna stiffened. "I only came to tell him to leave me alone—"

"Not to talk about marrying him in order to help his run for political office?"

Shock at how much Damon knew froze her in place. Guilty heat burned her cheeks, despite the fact that he had gotten the facts horribly wrong. "I have no intention of marrying Brad. Unless you haven't noticed, I'm already married to you!"

"You are married to me, at least for two months. And I was beginning to think you were happy with that—"

"I am! You know I am."

"Then why meet Henderson. *Here?*" Damon jerked his head in the direction of Tiffany's. "Looks like he's still waiting in line."

Jenna logged the display of engagement rings and suddenly understood why Brad had wanted the meeting there, *knowing* that he was being followed by a private detective.

Knowing that Damon would arrive.

Maybe he had genuinely wanted to get her back if he could, and the setup was aimed at encouraging her marriage with Damon to fall apart. Not that it needed much encouragement! Whatever he had intended, it was beginning to look like he had inflicted maximum damage.

"There's no line," she said flatly. "I only met Brad out of courtesy because at one stage I thought he would help me out by taking a partnership at Beaumont Law—"

"The partnership that I put one of my lawyers into."

Jenna frowned. Now he was making it sound like she had married him for Beaumont Law, which was what she had encouraged him to believe, even though it wasn't the truth!

She dragged in a breath. Her heart was pounding way too fast, and she was tense and on edge, because she had the horrible conviction that Damon really did think she was that manipulative when all she'd been was desperate.

Lifting her chin, she met his gaze. "Our marriage *was* a business deal. One *you* arranged. If you want the truth, the reason I went into it was because I wanted it to be real. But how can it be if you don't trust me? Now I'm beginning to feel that all I've done is make another mistake."

It was on the tip of her tongue to blurt out that she was pregnant with his child. Just a few minutes ago, she'd been dying to tell him the news, but now she didn't want to, because the knowledge was precious.

She'd been hugging it to herself for the last hour, and she couldn't bear it if he thought she had been manipulative about getting pregnant, too!

"If you'll excuse me," she said bleakly, "I need to get back to work."

Feeling sick to her stomach, she turned on her heel and walked away. Only this time she felt sick for real.

She made it to the ladies' room just in time as her stomach stopped threatening and began to heave. When she came out of the stall, she felt limp. A quick glance in the mirror told her that she looked washed-out.

She rinsed her face, patted it dry with a hand towel then leaned on the counter for long moments. An older woman gave her a sympathetic look. "Pregnant?"

"Yes." A little miserably, it occurred to her that the first person she had told about the pregnancy was a stranger, not Damon.

But after the way he had interrogated her—the things he had assumed about her—she *couldn't* have told him about a baby she had conceived in love. Given his suspicions, it even occurred to her that Damon might even question her motives for having unprotected sex with him, and she couldn't bear that, either.

In a moment of clarity, she understood that Damon's reaction was a result of the scars of his past. She knew something of his story, knew his mother had abandoned him, that he'd had a tough time with his father and that he had consciously avoided intimacy for years.

He'd been hurt over a long period of time, so of course he didn't want to risk that kind of hurt again. But that didn't help her, because she needed him to trust her—and to love her back.

More than that, she needed him to love their baby, and now she wasn't sure that he ever could.

Straightening, she picked up her bag and headed for the door. She would tell Damon about the baby eventually, but right now, hands down, she needed some time out. And in that moment her decision was made.

She needed to leave. She didn't know for how long, because she had a business to run, but right now she couldn't live with someone who believed she was cold and calculating and more interested in deals than a real relationship.

Someone who would never allow himself to truly love her.

Fifteen

Jaw tight, Damon strode into his office, barely noticing the hustle and bustle of admin staff or the cheerful greeting of his PA, Liz. Closing the door of his office behind him, he walked to the huge windows that occupied one wall and gazed unseeingly at the spectacular view of downtown Houston.

He had a brief flash of the way Jenna had looked at him just before she had walked away. Her face had been pale, her eyes dark. It occurred to him that at no point had she looked like a woman who was engaged in a romantic tryst or a businesslike arrangement with Henderson, and suddenly the feeling in his gut—the kind of feeling he usually didn't ignore—surfaced again.

Something was wrong.

Six years ago, Jenna had run straight into his arms to avoid her parents maneuvering her into Henderson's. Added to that, the only time he had seen her voluntarily touch Henderson had been on the main street of Ransom, when he knew she had deliberately used him to make Damon jealous.

For her to allow him into her life now was…wrong.

Damon shook his head. He felt like a haze was lifting.

He hadn't made a mistake about Henderson, who was a player from way back, but he was now certain he had made a mistake about Jenna and, now that he'd cooled off, the logic seemed clear.

It was a fact that if Jenna had wanted Henderson at any stage, like a lot of the other wealthy, privileged men she had dated, she could have gotten him. Six years ago, Henderson had tried to get her and failed, and even though he'd stayed in touch with Jenna, she hadn't let him close *until she'd gotten desperate about Beaumont Law.*

And any ideas that Jenna would marry anyone, including him, for money were patently wrong, because he had run into her in Houston any number of times when he did have wealth, and she hadn't shown a flicker of interest. It hadn't been until he had arranged the marriage with Chloe that she had come at him with all guns blazing—*to protect Chloe*, not because she had wanted him.

She had also been clear about not wanting payment for the marriage, or accepting the expensive SUV, which was, pointedly, still sitting, untouched, in his garage. All she'd accepted from him were the rings, and he was aware that accepting those had been an intensely feminine and emotional decision.

His fingers tightened into fists. She had wanted them because they were a visible sign that she was married to him.

And because she had wanted what he had always held back from giving her—the pent-up love and need he had locked away since he was twelve, because he couldn't risk walking that way again; he couldn't risk the rejection.

But the one thing he hadn't ever meant to do was inflict pain on Jenna, and this time he had.

He'd been wrong about her, on a whole lot of levels. Because it had been easier to find reasons to push her away—anything but let her in close and get hurt.

Although it was too late to avoid that, he thought grimly.

Taking his cell out of his pocket, he called Nick.

The conversation was brief. Nick had sent him a full report, most of which Damon knew, but one fact stood out. Jenna had repeatedly told Henderson to stop calling and texting, *because she was married to Damon.*

After hanging up, he rose to his feet and paced his office, ending up staring out across Houston's cityscape. Tension was humming through him.

Why hadn't Jenna told him Henderson was harassing her so he could have dealt with him?

The answer bounced back at him almost right away. Why would she tell him when she was used to living alone, running her own life and dealing with her own problems?

And when their marriage was only supposed to be a two months' business deal and he hadn't made one voluntary step toward changing it into the relationship she wanted.

Jaw tight, he slid his cell out of his pocket and called Jenna. When she didn't answer, he left a brief message asking her to call him back. He tried again, just in case she'd missed his initial call, then gave up.

On impulse, he dialed her business number. When the receptionist picked up, he was informed that Jenna had gone home and wouldn't be back in the office today.

With sudden decision, Damon rang through to Liz and told her he was going home early. Collecting his briefcase, he took the elevator down to the parking garage. Minutes later, he was in traffic. Another call to Jenna confirmed that she was not picking up his calls.

But why would she, when he had just accused her of lining up another marriage with Henderson and, by implication, of only marrying him because of what she could get out of the deal.

Damon stopped for lights, impatience making him tense, because he had the feeling that Jenna going home straight from the altercation at the Galleria was not a good sign. The lights turned green. Damon crawled forward in thickening traffic, his impatience building.

He was beginning to have the feeling that he was moving too slowly, that he was going to be too late.

That Jenna was leaving him.

Jenna drove into the River Oaks garage and quickly walked upstairs. She could hear Consuelo outside, probably talking to her husband, who was working in the garden, which suited her. All she wanted to do was pack and leave, quickly, because she didn't know what time Damon would get home.

She got her bag out of the closet and tossed clothes in, then did the same with the things in the dresser. A quick sweep through the bathroom and she had all her personal items. She remembered to unplug her phone charger from the wall and toss that in her case, then closed it up.

After storing her suitcase in the trunk of her rented SUV, she got behind the wheel and saw her rings.

Jaw set, she slid them off her finger and marched back upstairs. She found the door to Damon's suite, walked in and dropped the rings on his bedside table.

She refused to wear the rings of a man who, after ten years, didn't know her.

And, if nothing else, seeing she had returned the rings might actually tell Damon something real and concrete about her: that she did not see marriage as a way to get a man to buy her expensive jewelry.

If she wanted jewelry, she was more than capable of buying it for herself.

Climbing behind the wheel of the SUV, she

backed out and drove down the driveway. She had already made calls to the office. She would stay in touch by Zoom and had asked a part-timer, Shana, to come in full-time for the next few days. Happily, she had cleared her list of wedding events that she was personally organizing for the next week, so she didn't have to feel too guilty.

Turning out of the drive, she accelerated into traffic. Seconds later, she stopped behind a truck at a set of lights. As she accelerated through the intersection, Damon's Jeep flowed past.

Her heart thumped hard in her chest. She couldn't help it, she looked, but, luckily, he was staring straight ahead and didn't see her.

Pulse racing wildly, she continued to drive. That had been close. If she had left just a minute later, she would have met Damon in the drive.

Damon parked in the garage. There was no sign of Jenna's rental, which wasn't a good sign. He checked the kitchen, which was where, if Jenna was home early, she could usually be found. The kitchen was empty, so he continued up to her room.

He knocked on the door. When there was no answer, he stepped inside.

The bedroom was empty, so he checked her bathroom. His stomach hollowed out as he noted the cleared vanity and the towels in the laundry basket. He was just about to leave when he saw a blue-and-white box in the trash basket.

Frowning as the word *pregnancy* jumped out

at him, he examined the box, which *was* a pregnancy test kit. He had thought it would be a couple of weeks, at least, before she would know, but a quick glance at the instructions and a check of the stick inside the box and his chest locked up.

Jenna was pregnant.

For long moments he couldn't breathe then a cold wave of misery flowed through him. He had felt that emotion before, and knew all too well what it was: loss.

Dropping the kit back in the trash, he strode back out to her room and checked the closet. It was empty.

For long moments he couldn't think. Too late to wish he hadn't lost his temper. But the second he'd seen Henderson with Jenna, the past had risen up and broken over him and he'd been swamped by memories he didn't want and the knowledge that had always haunted him—that Jenna needed someone softer, easier, more *acceptable* than him.

Although that had never stopped him wanting her.

Because he loved her.

He drew a deep breath. He was *in love* with her, he corrected. And he had been for ten years.

That was why he hadn't been able to settle for anyone else and why he had pushed her away, because falling in love with Jenna had made him vulnerable in a way he had sworn he would never be again.

He'd buried the reasons why he didn't want intimacy, but Jenna had kept pushing past his barriers and breaking down his carefully constructed walls.

Now he had driven her away *for the fourth time*, and he didn't know if he could get her back.

And he wanted her back, he thought fiercely.

With a baby on the way, whether she would take him back or not, he needed to make amends. If she no longer wanted him in his life, he would accept her decision. But, at the very least, he wanted to offer her the support she needed through her pregnancy and when she had the baby.

His baby.

The thought struck him forcibly. Somehow, in the midst of everything that had gone wrong, they had made a child together, and he would not step back from that responsibility. He knew all too well what abandonment felt like. He would not do that to his own child.

He tried to call Jenna again. When it went through to voice mail, he tried the landline at her apartment. That also went through to voice mail. On impulse, he hit Chloe's number. If anyone knew where Jenna was, she would.

Seconds later, Chloe picked up.

"Before I tell you where Jenna might be," she said bluntly, "you need to tell me what's gone wrong, because Jenna will kill me for giving you the address."

Briefly, Damon filled her in on the background with Henderson.

"But you've got to know that Jenna doesn't even *like* Brad! The guy is a total pain. She was just looking for a lawyer to take over Beaumont Law until Luke could get there. I lost count of the number of lawyers she interviewed. She didn't contact Brad until she was, literally, desperate."

"There's one more thing. Jenna's pregnant."

There was a tense silence. "Okay," Chloe muttered, as if she had finally made up her mind. "You won't find her at her apartment; she's gone out of state. I'll give you the address on condition that you marry her."

"We are married," Damon said grimly.

"Well then, you need to marry her *properly*, because that matters. Caleb's on notice to marry me, and before our baby's born, otherwise, as far as I'm concerned, there won't *be* a wedding. Here's the phone number, and an address. It's her mother's farmhouse in Greensberg, Louisiana, not far from Baton Rouge. It's isolated and rural, and it's not in good repair, but it's the one piece of her mother's inheritance that Jenna hung on to for herself. And that's one thing you have to know about Jenna. She's about *family*, first, last and always, not business."

Once he'd noted the details down, Damon thanked Chloe and terminated the call. If Jenna was going to Louisiana, then she was flying, so he found the number for the airport and checked flights. There was a flight leaving from Bush Intercontinental Airport in an hour's time. It was the last one today, so the chances were that was the flight Jenna had taken.

Damon strode to his room and grabbed the fresh clothes he would need. As he was about to walk out of the room, the afternoon sun picked up the glitter of something on his bedside table.

Jenna's rings.

He picked up the engagement ring and the diamond-studded band that went with it. He should have expected it, he thought bleakly.

The rings were a clear message that, as far as Jenna was concerned, they might still be legally married, but their relationship was over.

Stowing the rings in his pocket, he picked up his overnight case and left the room.

As he loaded his bag into the Jeep, fragments of the past kept surfacing. In the years he had kept tabs on her, none of the men she'd dated—wealthy, eligible men—had ever gotten more than two dates, max. For someone who had been brought up in a Southern family that made a business out of marrying well, that statistic was definitive.

And, in that moment, another facet of Jenna's personality fell into place, because he was abruptly sure that she hadn't let anyone close *but him*.

She had hinted, and it had been right before his nose, but he had been too busy pushing Jenna away to recognize it.

He knew she had been a virgin the first time they had made love. The second time they had gotten together, she had made a point of telling him that she hadn't slept with anyone else. Three months ago had been different. Jenna had been quieter, more reserved; all she'd done was ask him to go slow, because she hadn't made love for a long time.

Every instinct told him that "a long time" had

meant six years, that Jenna had been referring to the last time *they* had made love.

Feeling sick to his stomach, Damon swung behind the wheel of the Jeep and drove.

As he negotiated traffic, which was starting to gridlock because it was almost five, he called the airline. It was looking like he wasn't going to get to the airport before Jenna went through the departure gate, so he needed to get a seat if that was still possible.

When the airline confirmed that the flight was completely booked, he called the jet charter firm he had used to fly from San Antonio to Houston, to check out their availability. After a frustrating wait while he was stuck in traffic, they confirmed that they could fly him to Baton Rouge and then on to an airport closer to Greensberg, but there would be a wait while the jet was fueled and the flight plan submitted.

Half an hour later, Damon reached the airport. A quick check of the departures board confirmed that boarding had closed: he was too late to catch Jenna.

Jaw taut, he took the stairs to the huge concourse with its viewing area and watched as the jet that likely held Jenna taxied down the runway then powered up into the sky.

She was gone, and it was his fault. He had been too focused on the scars of his past—on keeping himself safe, *and alone*—and she had finally had enough. The miracle of it was that she had let him close at all.

But that was also why he would not give up on her now.

She had given him more chances than he deserved, and every time he had taken her softness and her love, and he had let her down.

But not any more. If nothing else, he was determined to tell her that he loved her.

More, that he needed her in his life.

If she would allow him back in.

Sixteen

It was almost midnight by the time Jenna arrived at the old Greensberg cottage, an antique remnant of her family's past that was tucked away in the rural countryside northeast of Baton Rouge.

As she parked the new SUV she'd rented in the gravel drive, despite feeling exhausted, she felt oddly calm, a state of mind that, weirdly, went hand in hand with finding out that she was pregnant.

As adrenaline-inducing as the knowledge had been, decision making had suddenly become simplified, because she was now living and planning for *two*. Her baby was depending on her, so she couldn't afford to mess up with Damon again.

They were over.

Misery shivered through her. But, as bleak as

that thought was, she had to accept it and move on. She didn't know how long it would take to get over Damon, because she had been in love with him for ten years, but she was out of choices: she had to try.

Leaving the SUV's lights on, she climbed out into the chilly autumnal air and took stock of the rambling two-story Victorian timber house, which, in the beams of the rental's headlights, looked just a little spooky. Thankfully, she had taken the time to change out of her work clothes into jeans and leather boots, a cashmere sweater, and a light coat, so she wasn't cold.

She found the house keys, looped the strap of her tote over one shoulder and grabbed one of the sacks of groceries she had bought from the local supermarket. Pausing under the inky shelter of the porch, she activated the light on her phone unlocked the door and pushed it open.

A wave of emotion washed through her as she stepped inside. It had been almost a year since she had last visited, so inside smelled stale and dusty, but that didn't change the fact that the house was a place filled with happy childhood memories.

Switching on the hall and porch lights, she walked through to the kitchen and dumped her bag and the groceries on the small oak kitchen table.

Once she'd ferried in the rest of the groceries and her luggage, she locked the SUV, then walked out to the garage and turned on the water supply and switched on the pump so there was water to the house.

With the wind shifting to northerly, it seemed a whole lot cooler. Luckily, there was still wood piled in the log basket beside the wood burner in the sitting room. Ten minutes shy of midnight, once the fire was going, she walked through to the kitchen and boiled some water to make chamomile tea. No more caffeine while she was pregnant.

Even though she shouldn't be hungry, because she had grabbed a snack dinner at the airport, she found a packet of crackers and some cheese slices and carried them, along with her tea, into the living room. Sitting beside the fire, with a blanket she had fetched from the linen cupboard over her knees, she sipped the steaming brew and munched crackers.

Her appetite, she noticed, was definitely weird now. She had been crazy hungry at the airport and had ended up buying things to eat that she *never* bought, like fries. Now, even though she should be happily replete, she wanted to eat again. Although maybe that had something to do with the fact that she had lost her lunch.

She got up to put another log on the fire and smothered a yawn. She should grab fresh sheets from the hall cupboard and make up a bed, but she felt too tired to move, so she simply sat down and watched the flames. As she began to doze, vivid memories of the confrontation with Damon flickered, shunting her back into hollow misery.

With an effort of will, she checked the emotion. She had been here before, she reminded herself. She knew what it felt like to be shut out, so there was no need to make herself feel worse.

The problem was, it had never felt quite so hopeless, and she had never felt so utterly rejected.

She awoke with a crick in her neck to find morning light filtering through the edges of the thick curtains, and the fire dead in the grate. She checked her watch. Amazingly, it was after seven.

Walking to the kitchen, she switched on the electric jug and retrieved her phone from her tote only to discover that she had forgotten to switch it off flight mode. As soon as she reactivated the phone, texts and notifications of missed calls flooded in, a number from Damon—which, unpalatably, made her heart leap—and a few from Chloe.

Resolutely ignoring his missed calls, she read the last text from Chloe, which had come through at around eleven last night, and her heart almost stopped in her chest. Chloe had given Damon her address; she was certain he was on his way, and now she was going crazy with worry and *why* wasn't Jenna answering her phone!

Stomach churning, Jenna worked her way through Damon's texts and voice mail messages. They were typically brief; he wanted to talk, he was sorry for what happened in the mall and was aware she probably didn't want to see him, but he was on his way to Greensberg, anyway.

Adrenaline pumped, banishing the last vestiges of sleepiness and making her heart pound. In all the time she had known Damon, through all their breakups, he had never, not once, come after her.

But it was *why* he was coming after her now that mattered.

If he simply wanted her back in his mansion as part of the marriage agreement, then she wasn't interested.

As far as she was concerned, she would stick by her agreement—she would stay married to Damon for two months. But as for the living together thing? Damon could fight that out in court with his uncle's lawyers. The way she saw it, their pregnancy was confirmation enough that the marriage *was* real.

Mind going a million miles an hour, she found the teapot and dropped in a chamomile tea bag. As she did so, she heard the low rumble of a vehicle. A quick check through the window and her heart went into overdrive again.

Damon had just pulled in behind her SUV, which meant he must have caught a red-eye flight or chartered a private jet, because she had gotten the last flight to Baton Rouge last night.

Feeling distinctly on edge, she twitched curtains open, letting more light in, and walked out to the hallway. On the way, she stopped to check her appearance in the small, old-fashioned mirror that hung on the wall.

Her hair was tousled from sleep and she was a little pale, but as from yesterday, looking good for Damon was not exactly a priority!

Damon studied the two-story timber house that looked like it was all of a hundred years old, and climbed out of the four-wheel-drive rental he had picked up after his jet had landed the previous night. Because it had been late when he'd gotten in, instead of driving on to Greensberg, he had stopped and spent the night in a motel.

The cottage, and the property, were so modest he was tempted to double-check the address on his navigational system, but the rental SUV parked directly in front of him informed him that he was at the right place.

As he walked up to the front porch, the door opened and Jenna stepped out. Damon halted at the bottom step. "Did you get my messages?"

She held up her phone. "About a minute ago."

Jenna's gaze held a steely edge he recognized. He had seen it when she had questioned his engagement to Chloe, then again when she had insisted on dragging out the wedding dress she had ended up wearing from her crashed SUV. "Can I come in?"

"Only if you promise not to insult me." Turning on her heel, she walked back inside.

Relieved that at least she'd consented to talk to him, Damon followed her inside to a small, cozy kitchen, and watched as she poured boiling water into a teapot.

Turning, she placed the teapot and two mugs on the table. After pouring what smelled like chamomile tea, something she'd encouraged him to drink in the evenings, she handed him a gently steaming mug. "Brad set me up."

"Yes, he did. He knew the PI would let me know

about the meeting, then made sure it was in front of a jeweler's."

She stared at him for a long moment then sat down. "Why didn't you know that yesterday?"

"Because I was crazy jealous. Henderson played me, and I fell for it." He met her gaze briefly. "I'm sorry. I guess, where you're concerned, I've always believed that you wouldn't stay."

She frowned. "How can you say that when I tried to get you *four* times—"

"And that there hasn't been anyone but me, ever."

She sent him a stark look. "I didn't think you had gotten that part."

Damon's gaze was sombre. "It took me a while, but I figured it out eventually." He set the steaming mug down on the table. What he had to say wasn't easy, and words were not exactly his forte, but he was fighting for his life here. "Your father had a couple of conversations with me, warning me off. The first when you were nineteen."

Her gaze flew to his. "I found that out, but only a few weeks ago. It would have been nice if *I'd* been included in one of those conversations."

"The point I'm trying to make," Damon said quietly, "is that I didn't finish with you each time we got together because I didn't want you. It was for the opposite reason."

She frowned. "Are you saying you wanted to marry me six years ago?"

"No," he said flatly. "Six years ago we would never have worked."

"Because you wanted to inherit first?"

"Because I was damaged goods, and I was set to walk down the same path as my father when Alan Wyatt intervened and gave me another life. The whole reason he wanted me to marry was because he was afraid I never would, and he was right. The last thing I wanted to do was let anyone get too close."

Jenna wrapped her fingers around her mug. "I remember your mother's family before they moved away. I guess it didn't help that I came out of the same country club set."

Damon shrugged. "My mother came from money, and she was a debutante. The plain fact was she couldn't take life with my father."

Or me.

The words remained unspoken, because they were words Damon never generally acknowledged, but he was beginning to realize that they sat at the heart of what was going wrong. He looked like his father, and he'd been afraid of *becoming* his father.

"But you're not your father," Jenna said softly, utterly surprising him.

For a split second Damon wondered if he'd inadvertently said the words out loud, or if she could read his mind. "I'm not now," he said grimly, and in that moment he recognized something he should have acknowledged a long time ago—that, years on, Alan Wyatt *had* succeeded. When he looked in the mirror, he no longer saw his father.

"You never were Cole Wyatt," Jenna said flatly. "I'm sorry, maybe I shouldn't have an opinion because he was your father, but I knew him, I heard the gossip and I saw him around. He was *exactly* the man he wanted to be. You are not like him—you never were. Why do you think I fell for you when I was nineteen?"

Damon stared at Jenna for a long moment, and something broke inside him. At a guess, it was another wall. "Nineteen?"

She shrugged. "I make up my mind fast. I wouldn't have slept with you if I hadn't been in love with you. That's not how I work. And why on earth do you think there's never been anyone else?"

There went another wall, Damon thought, but he couldn't regret it because he could see Jenna's heart in her eyes and, out of nowhere hope swelled. "So… where are we now?"

Jenna rose to her feet, too on edge to sit. She had loved her father to pieces, but she had known what he was like—a traditionalist with strong opinions. No matter how decent or hardworking Damon was, her father would only have seen him as the son of Cole Wyatt, a gambler and a drunk who was regularly locked up for brawling.

Her mother's position, as a force on the Southern debutante circuit had been even more clear-cut. From the time Jenna had been born, Catherine Beaumont had been plotting her only daughter's course into a very good marriage.

She knew the obstacles Damon had faced, but she had faced them, too, in different ways. She *got* him.

And she was happy he had apologized, but there was still an empty ache in her heart, because they were still a long way from the happy, in-love relationship she wanted.

He now knew she loved him, and he knew what she wanted, but he was still a frustrating enigma to her.

And there was still another huge issue to overcome. If he couldn't love her, hands down, she would not subject this baby to a loveless marriage. She had chosen to risk herself for Damon, and she had gotten *hurt*. She would not risk her child. She drew a deep breath. "I'm pregnant."

His gaze locked with hers. "I know. I found the test kit in your bathroom."

It was the last thing she expected to hear, but it filled her with the first dizzy glimmerings of hope, because only a man bent on commitment would chase after a pregnant woman. "I'm only just pregnant," she said cautiously, finding herself rushing into words, because she was suddenly wildly nervous. "It might not go full term. Sometimes—"

"I hope it does," he said fiercely. "I want our baby."

She drew a sharp breath. *"Why?"*

He rose to his feet. "Because I love you. Truth be told, I've loved you for years, I just didn't want to admit it, because I didn't think there could be a future—"

An almost painful, out-of-control happiness swelled in her heart. "Say the 'I love you' bit again."

"I love you," he said simply. "And I'll love our child, *if* you'll let me be a part of your lives."

"Yes," she said simply, her throat closing up, because those were the words she'd needed, and then there was no time to talk, because he pulled her close, wrapping her tight.

Long minutes later, he loosened his hold. "There's just one more thing. If we're doing this, we need to get married again, and this time, we're going to do it properly."

He went down on one knee, reached into his pocket and produced two very familiar rings. Grasping her left hand, he met her gaze, his heart in his eyes. "Jenna Evelyn Wyatt, will you marry me, again?"

Tears filming her eyes, she answered, "I will."

He slipped the engagement ring on her finger and slipped the wedding ring back in his pocket, signaling that it was reserved for another, very special day.

And just like that, she had it all—the gorgeous guy, the wedding of her dreams to look forward to and the icing on the cake: their baby on the way.

Epilogue

The wedding happened fast.

Since she was pregnant, there was no time to waste, because no way did she want to look like she'd put on weight in her wedding photos. And since she was an industry insider, she was able to wangle the church she wanted, cut to the front of the line and get the dresses made and fitted in time, and lock in hairdressers, manicurists…the whole kit and caboodle.

Megan was her maid of honor; Chloe and two of the other girls from work, Tess and Zara, were bridesmaids; and Luke had taken time off from Harvard to give her away.

It went without saying that her dress was a Vera Wang, and she had gone for broke this time, with a princess dress in pure white silk, with lace and bling from Africa and a gorgeous veil that swept down her back. The roses in her bouquet were white with touches of pink and were beautifully offset with glossy green leaves.

Everything was *perfect*.

Just minutes before she was due to leave, there was a knock on her door. Megan opened it and almost had a fit, because it was Damon.

His dark eyes locked on hers and Jenna drew in her breath. Last night she'd had a bachelorette party, and she'd spent the night with Megan, so she hadn't seen Damon for almost twenty-four hours, which, apparently, was the whole point. In a morning suit, Damon looked gorgeous.

He glanced at her maid of honor. "Can I have a moment?"

Predictably, Megan melted. Within seconds the room was cleared.

Jenna pushed to her feet, careful not to trip on all the silk and tulle. "Megan's right. You're *not* supposed to be here."

Damon stared at her for a long moment. "You look…beautiful, but then you always do. I've got something I've been keeping for a while. I was hoping you might like to wear them today."

Reaching inside the jacket of his suit, he took out a long jewelry box decorated with the Ambrosi crest. Setting the box down on her dressing table, he opened it, and her breath caught in her throat.

Nestled in oyster silk were a set of pear-shaped diamond earrings and a matching pendant and bracelet, the bespoke jewels that went with her engagement ring.

With fingers that shook slightly, she fastened the bracelet, then took out the diamond studs she was wearing and inserted the diamond drops.

She drew in her breath. "They are…gorgeous."

Damon lifted the pendant, which looked even more delicate in his big hands, and fastened it around her neck. As she looked at her reflection, with Damon standing behind her, looking broad and darkly handsome, her heart swelled and tears misted her eyes. Lately the pregnancy had been making her wildly emotional. For a person who didn't cry, suddenly she was crying at the drop of a hat. "When did you get them?"

He turned her around, his fingers threading with hers. "The same day we got the engagement ring. I knew they'd look gorgeous on you, and I wanted to make up for how insensitive I'd been, so I got Bruno to courier them over to the house later."

"I *love* them." And he had loved her all along— he just hadn't admitted it.

Jenna hugged him. Weirdly, she found hugging Damon was the way to intimacy, not kissing. Although kissing was nice, too. And she was beginning to learn that the things she'd thought weren't loving about Damon, like his not being able to resist her and wanting to beat Brad up on her behalf, were actually his way of expressing love. You live and learn.

But, happily, with her help, Damon was now learning a more positive language of love, which he then expressed for about five minutes until Megan practically broke the door down.

An hour later, her limousine pulled up at the beautiful St. John the Divine church, not far from the River Oaks mansion. Luke, looking tall and handsome and bursting with pride in his gray suit, held out his arm and walked her slowly in.

As they paused in the vestibule, she thought briefly back to the wedding at the Pleasant River Lodge. This one couldn't be more different. For a start, the sun was shining, and the church was filled with the light that flowed through the tall windows. Roses decorated the ends of the pews, and candles flickered, filling the air with the scent of honey.

As the strains of the wedding march started, Luke smiled down at her, hugging her close for a moment, then they began the slow walk down the aisle. As they did so, Damon, flanked by his best man, Caleb, and three groomsmen, turned. His gaze connected with hers, and her heart swelled.

In the last few weeks, their relationship had flourished. With the whole emotional roller coaster of being in love solved, they had both finally managed to relax, and they were slowly learning each other and how to fit their lives together.

Three weeks ago, they had taken time out and had had a week's holiday in San Francisco, touring vineyards, sitting in cafés and doing all the goofy tourist things. And of course, lately, they had been redecorating the room next to the master bedroom as a nursery.

As they reached the altar, dark oak with a simple gold cross, suspended in a beam of light, Luke handed her to Damon. As she placed her hands in his, for a moment her composure wobbled, but then his gaze locked with hers, he smiled, and she steadied.

The priest began, and the ebb and flow of the sacred wrapped them in timeless words. When they exchanged gold bands and the priest announced that Damon could kiss her, finally this part of the journey seemed complete, even as another was starting.

Finally she had the man of her dreams, and together, they were going to have the baby.

Now the wedding was perfect, and they were playing by the real marriage rules.

The rules of love.

* * * * *

*If you loved this book by Fiona Brand,
don't miss her Pearl House series!*

A Breathless Bride
A Tangled Affair
A Perfect Husband
The Fiancée Charade
Just One More Night
The Sheik's Pregnancy Proposal
Needed: One Convenient Husband
Keeping Secrets
Twin Scandals
How to Live with Temptation

#2869 STAKING A CLAIM

Texas Cattleman's Club: Ranchers and Rivals • by Janice Maynard

With dreams of running the family ranch, Layla Grandin has no time for matchmaking. Then, set up with a reluctant date, Layla realizes he sent his twin instead! Their attraction is undeniable but, when the ranch is threatened, can she afford distractions?

#2870 LOST AND FOUND HEIR

Dynasties: DNA Dilemma • by Joss Wood

Everything is changing for venture capitalist Garrett Kaye—he's now the heir to a wealthy businessman *and* the company's next CEO. But none of this stops him from connecting with headstrong Jules Carson. As passions flare, will old wounds and new revelations derail everything?

#2871 MONTANA LEGACY

by Katie Frey

After the loss of his brother, rancher Nick Hartmann is suddenly the guardian of his niece. Enter Rose Kelly—the new tutor. Sparks fly, but with his ranch at stake and the secrets she's keeping, there's a lot at risk for them both...

#2872 ONE NIGHT EXPECTATIONS

Devereaux Inc. • by LaQuette

Successful attorney Amara Devereaux-Rodriguez is focused on closing her family's multibillion dollar deal. But then she meets Lennox Carlisle, the councilman and mayoral candidate who stands in their way. He's hard to resist. And one hot night together leads to a little surprise neither expected...

#2873 BLACK TIE BACHELOR BID

Little Black Book of Secrets • by Karen Booth

To build her boutique hotel, socialite Taylor Klein needs reclusive hotelier Roman Scott—even if that means buying his "date" at a charity bachelor auction. She wins the bid and a night with him, but will the sparks between them upend her goals?

#2874 SECRETS OF A WEDDING CRASHER

Destination Wedding • by Katherine Garbera

Hoping for career advancement, lobbyist Melody Conner crashes a high-profile wedding to meet with Senator Darien Bisset. What she didn't expect was to spend the night with him. There's a chemistry neither can deny, but being together could upend all their professional goals...

A sharp rap on her door startled Arlie out of her misery.

"Just a minute!" she called, twisting off the shower.

Opening the shower door, she slid into one of the complimentary plush robes, then gathered the long skein of her hair and squeezed the water out of it with a towel before draping it over her shoulder.

Good enough for food delivery. She exited the bathroom in a cloud of steam and pulled open the propped door.

Samuel Kane's face appeared in the gap.

Only he didn't look like Samuel Kane.

He looked like wrath in a Brooks Brothers suit. Jaw set, the muscles flexed, mouth a thin, grim line. Eyes blazing emerald against chiseled cheekbones.

"Oh," she said dumbly. "Hi."

A sinking feeling of self-consciousness further heated her already shower-warmed skin as he stared at her.

"Do you want to come in?" she added when he made no reply. She stepped aside to grant him entry, catching the subtle scent of him as he moved past her into the hallway.

"Why didn't you tell me?" he asked.

Arlie's heart sank into her guts. There were too many answers to this question. And too many questions he didn't even know to ask.

"Tell you what?" she asked, opting for the safest path.

Coward.

Samuel stepped closer, her glowing white robe reflected in icy arcs in his glacier-green eyes. "About my father. About what he said to you this morning."

The wave of relief was so complete and acute it actually weakened her knees.

"Our families have a lot of shared history," Arlie said. "Not all of it good."

"He had no right—"

"I'm sorry," she interrupted, knowing it was a weak and deliberate dodge. She didn't want to talk about this. Not with him. "It's absolutely mandatory that you surrender your tie and suit jacket for this conversation. I'm entirely underdressed and frankly feeling a little vulnerable about it."

Walking into the well-appointed sitting area, Samuel shrugged out of his suit jacket and laid it across the chaise longue. As he turned, they snagged gazes. He gripped the knot of his tie, loosening it with small deliberate strokes that inexplicably kindled heat between Arlie's thighs.

"Better?" he asked.

On a different night, in a different universe, it would have ended there.

But for reasons she could neither explain nor ignore, Arlie padded barefoot across the space between them.

"Almost." Lifting her hands to his neck, she undid the button closest to his collar. Then another. And another.

To her great surprise and delight, Samuel wore no T-shirt beneath.

Dizzy with desire, Arlie tilted her face up to his. The air was alive with electricity, crackling and sizzling with anticipation. The breathless inevitability of this thing between them made her feel loose-limbed and drunk.

"All my life, I could have anything I wanted." Cupping her jaw, he ran the pad of his thumb over her lower lip. "Except you."

Arlie's breath came in irregular bursts, something deep inside her tightening at his admission. "You want me?"

Samuel only looked at her, silent but saying all.

His wordlessness the purest part of what he had always given her.

The look that passed between them was both question and answer.

Yes?

Yes.

Don't miss what happens next in…
Corner Office Confessions
by USA TODAY *bestselling author Cynthia St. Aubin.*

Available May 2022 wherever
Harlequin Desire books and ebooks are sold.

Harlequin.com